NARTHEX

AND OTHER STORIES

T0163056

NARTHEX
AND OTHER STORIES

H.D.

WITH AN AFTERWORD BY MICHAEL BOUGHN

BookThug · 2011

FIRST BOOKTHUG EDITION

"Ear-ring" was first published in *Life and Letters Today* 14.4 (Summer 1936)
under the name D. A. Hill.
"Pontikinisi (Mouse Island)" was first published in *Pagany* 3.3 (July-September 1932)
under the name Rhoda Peters.
"Narthex" was first publiahed in *The Second American Caravan*, ed. Alfred Kreymborg,
Lewis Mumford, and Paul Rosenfeld. NY: Macaulay Co, 1928.

Thanks to Victor Coleman for transcribing the original texts.

for Harvey Brown, wherever

LIBRARY AND ARCHIVES CANADA CATALOGUING IN PUBLICATION

H.D. (Hilda Doolittle), 1886–1961
Narthex & other stories / H.D. (Hilda Doolittle) ; edited,
with an afterword, by Michael Boughn.

(Department of reissue; no. 8)
Contents: Ear-ring – Pontikinisi (Mouse Island) – Narthex.
ISBN 978-1-897388-96-9

I. Boughn, Michael II. Title. III. Series: Department of reissue ; no. 8

PS3507.O726A6 2011   813.52   C2011-904778-0

PRINTED IN CANADA

CONTENTS

EAR-RING

SOMEONE HAD BOUGHT her with two diamonds and she carried that implication with her, as heads, self-consciously and a shade too indifferently, did not turn towards her. One sensed her coming (it was the same, last night) but having had two nights of exactly this same entrance, Madelon Thorpe felt slightly immunized against it. She thought, this is my third night in Athens. Madelon measured time by those diamonds, they stressed something, were other than they appeared (don't look at her), were shriek-marks obviously, were paperweights, set at two corners of the billowing fabric of her perception of this ball-room, dining-room of the *Hôtel Acropole et Angleterre,* embossed in gold letters on the menu. Madelon measured time by those stones; I have been here three days, I sailed from the port of London to the port of Athens; it must be now nearly a month since we left. One had to hold on to something.

Archie Rowe was their guest, Eleanor's guest that is, I am Eleanor Eddington's guest. If only Eleanor wouldn't hunch forward so (she thought of her as "Eleanor" in this milieu, rather than "E.E." or "Edd," as she had learned to call her). If only Eleanor wouldn't leave everything to me. Archie Rowe, half-Greek, had the most fantastic ideas of how people from London should act. Here, everyone knew everything. Dare she ask about the diamonds? He would make no obvious comment. She must wait patiently. The diamonds were cutting into circles of small-talk; compact, magnetic centres, grouped about small tables, and, at intervals, larger tables, by some law of common gravitation, gravitated from them. They might be divided in everything, upper, lower and middle parties, royalists and Venizelists, but by some unwritten pact, transcending the mere manifestoes of kings and emperors, they were banded together against this; this not too attractive, not too un-attractive visitor from beyond the Black Sea. Though almost all were visitors, they revolved in their various circles (small tables and larger, set at intervals), away, at least, from this. In their incredible disparities and antipathies, social, racial and political, they were held together by one thing – their aloofness from the diamonds.

The diamonds, rather than the woman who wore them, sought recognition. Or were the diamonds arrogant in their indifference, did they, by some occult power, drive these human entities to shun them? Archie Rowe would have their history. They might have been gouged out, *en passant,* from a royal diadem, or, equally, they might have been filched from some sacrosanct Byzantine shrine. Or, even more astonishingly, they might have been the exact and peculiar property of the taller partner, a stolid bulk of broadcloth that followed the satin sheath, above which rose a head, a catastrophe, pale and cut-off and un-related to the body, swathed in black, beneath it. The head was, in no way, remarkable. Madelon (not looking at it) remembered it from last night, from the night before last. The shoulders and the head were a marble cast, Clyte, set on a black stand; this head would revolve, if the base were edged slightly to left, to right. Almost, one felt, the bulkier attendant, who might

8

be equally a butler or a grand-duke, was curator of this question-able treasure – a not very good head, done in inferior marble, of a second-rate Clyte. The hair, loose above the temples, was of no special period; late Edwardian might suggest it. The black velvet band, at the throat, suggested a crack in the bust that had not been adequately mended. Altogether, the thing was not worth looking at; an unwritten yet overstressed social law decreed, moreover, that one should not look.

THE DIAMONDS WERE, unquestionably, out of all proportion, but it couldn't be just that. Archie Rowe, assuredly, had chapter and verse up his sleeve. The pair drawn, so to speak, in the wake of those stones, might be anybody. But where everybody was some-body, and all non-relatedly and extravagantly individual, how did it happen that these two, dressed in black, correct in all their at-titudes, attracted this sort of implied and negative attention? The waiters had left a narrow gangway. But between their row and that other set of tables, shoved, in intimate irregularity, against a dark maroon curtain, ran Lethe or Styx. Was it just the diamonds did it? Whose were they? Who had worn them? They were search-lights. Revolving lights, from a squat lighthouse, cut across small tables and larger tables, all of whose personal individualities were magne-tized to this one point, their supreme indifference. Whatever they might whisper furtively, hiding a cough, as it were, behind a napkin, be sure it was not diamonds. Did Madelon imagine it? It seemed the negation of their impression was focusing it all in her direction. She would be fused herself, to a common centre (if she did not dodge their influence, like these others) and be burnt up by them.

But this was ridiculous. She was giving them undue value. There was so much else to think of. Talk ran high; no matter how decorous the undertone, one felt there was some high voltage, some high-explosive power, about the simplest utterance. One almost saw glitter of epigram, running like a magnesium flare from table to table; large table-circles and smaller circles, seemed to repeat collective messages, in different languages. There was incredible babel of tongues; each cut across the other, French, English, English-French, French-English. Occasionally, there was an unpredictable guttural undertone; somewhere, just beneath them, must be the Dutch ambassador, for Archie Rowe was saying, "Miss Eddington, there's a dance tomorrow at the Dutch Legation, do you care for dancing?"

Talk about anything but the diamonds. The woman was about to sit down. Certainly, I don't know what it's all about, but someone must look at her. It makes it too important that no one should look. Almost, as if mesmerized by the diamonds, Madelon looked up. There was nothing new in this sight. The black, rather heavy, broad-cloth shoulders of the male partner were, as usual, inclined slightly as he waited for his companion to be seated. The black satin sheath was without wrinkle or fold, as if an expert lady's maid had, just this moment, run an iron across it. The sheath wrinkled in parallel lines, as a knee bent slightly. The owner of the diamonds shoved a knee round the edge of the table, finding a foot-hold, the other side of Lethe. Across Styx, she flung out a smile.

NOBODY ANSWERED THE smile. The petroleum magnate, just above the diamonds, went on talking to his secretary. She always wore the same hat. From time to time, she affectedly dipped its forward-set willow-plume across her eyes, and as affectedly, flung it back. She and the wife of the military attaché from Washington, always wore their hats. Petroleum and attaché sat above Eleanor, Archie Rowe and Madelon; almost at their elbow, the other side, sat England talking French to somebody, with morose almond eyes, who might be Persian. A girl, alone at a table, had been pointed out, at lunch time, as relief-committee back from Serbia. Dutch a bit lower down, and another guttural. Beyond, was the edge of no-man's-land, people even Archie Rowe couldn't find time to bow to. And all talking and no one talking, she felt certain, about diamonds. Eleanor, at last, realizing that mischief might be done here and Archie Rowe might be annoyed, was now patiently staring at them. Madelon, having all but smiled at the diamond, now in question, thought she might as well say something. She formed a question, with half-open lips, which Archie fearfully interrupted, "Ah – " as he let slide his shallow soup-spoon, he turned sideways to take the wine list from the waiter, and breathed rather than whispered, "fabulous Wr-ussians."

They must be that, certainly.

What Russian was not fabulous, who had escaped a red revolution by way of a black sea, moreover, complete with diamonds? There was no other possible Russian in this hotel, perhaps not in the whole world. Say "Russian" and you say "fabulous." Archie had told them nothing. He seemed to sense everything, separately, from the two sides of his face, like a fish.

THE DIAMONDS DIMINISHED. One was cut off by the pink lamp-shade; identical lamps were set on all their tables. The diamond hung, glittering in space, against the dark maroon curtain. It was laid vertical on dark velvet, like a diamond in a show-case, reversing the commonplaces of mere gravity. It should fall down or they should fall down or they should fall up. War dizziness and late London war and a trip, but three days finished, on a winter sea, from the port of London to the port of Athens, made all this feasible. Everything, in this back-water, left by the high tide of events, went round in concentric circles. Only the diamond remained static, it was the centre of a mystical circle, a problem out of geometry. The upside-down museum case held a head, now she thought of it, guillotined by a narrow bank of black velvet (French revolution, Russian revolution); it seemed the only reality in the surcharged atmosphere of a room, where everything might, at any moment, slip over the edge of nothing into nowhere. Hold on to something. Archie was naming various notables to Eleanor, indicating their whereabouts, with an inclination of a shoulder or almost imperceptible jerk of an elbow. He covered even these slightest of indiscretions, by side-talk in Greek to a waiter; his words, now as she attended to them, seemed to merge into the syllables of that pair, across the narrow aisle. Russian and modern Greek – was there so much to choose between them?

Where there were so many questions to be asked, why not stick, as everyone else seemed bent on ignoring it, to the most obvious? Where did the diamonds come from? People, even Russians, even in nineteen-twenty, didn't go about, even in Athens, wearing jewels, like roc's eggs, in their ears.

MADELON SAID a number to herself, thought "nineteen-twenty," and already, the hard fact of four decisive numbers in a row (1-9-2-0) had jerked her into some feasible contact with these others. She repeated the number to herself, across the laboured witticisms of Archie Rowe, at the expense of the late head of the British school of Athens. The discreet jibe was carefully calculated to reach the ears of the present head of the school, who was, Archie had earlier informed them, the owner of the somewhat coffin-like, somewhat something-in-the-diplomatic set of shoulders, two tables beyond them, to his left. Was this arrangement of tables carefully calculated, or were they all dumped down, anywhere? Certainly, it would be assumed that they, personally, were above the salt, but then, how did those particular Russians happen to have snaffled that desirable corner table? Or was it all chance? There did seem, it is true, a sort of loose logic in the arrangement of their neighbours, this side of the aisle. They were all, so to speak, English speaking, a mixed, to be sure, bag, but differentiated somehow from Balkans, Russians, native Greeks, visiting Roumanians; the inhabitants of the lower half of the room were frankly indefinable. The Russians with the diamonds seemed to be the high-water mark of the Balkan tide-wave. Nineteen-twenty, Madelon repeated, like some abracadabra (1-9-2-0), a charm to make this snap into some proportion. I am in Athens, she said to herself, and this is nineteen-twenty; she repeated it like a telephone number.

Now, as she said to herself, it took form. Madelon found she had something else to hold to, beside diamonds. One, nine, two, O. Write it in a row, like a sum from the baby-arithmetic, or write it, with dashes in between, like a Morse-code signal. It was some sort of signal. Everything in the world had gone down, in a vortex of babel-tongues, long since. This was a whirl-pool in a back-wash, something, in miniature, of what that had been. It was a relic; already, in nineteen-twenty, pre-war. Pre-merry-widow at that.

The crowd looked, for all its casual appearance, like a carefully arranged curtain for an opera-bouffe finale. But it is something quite different; really, she thought, it is chemistry, it is pure geometry. They were a fabulous mixture, altogether, in a test-tube (that hotel ball-room). Little tables and larger seemed to seethe, each with its particular alchemic property. The diamonds were two radium-points of something indissoluble, where everything else was seething. The rest of the mixture, vibrated away, in chemical disapprobation, would have nothing to do with them. "Prophilia?" asked Archie Rowe, with a slightly quizzical inflection, as if to remind her where she was, dragging her back from diamonds.

"OH YES," she said quickly, "thank you so much. I like it so much." She had said all this before, she knew exactly what she would say, she knew he would say, "Do you like the *retsinato?*" Even before he spoke the word, she knew he was going to ask if they liked the resinous Greek wine, as if she were thinking for him, for herself. It was a commonplace question here, and it had a commonplace answer, yet as she said it, she seemed to have been saying it over and over, all her life, with no interim, of boats and ports, and blue hyacinths in a basket, at Gibraltar. She knew she had to say it, so she said it, "It takes *time* to get used to it. It has a special sort of *tang*, hasn't it? I mean, after one *has* got used to it," etcetera. She was saying it for Eleanor. Why didn't Eleanor speak up, say her own lines? She drags me into this startling milieu and just leaves me to flounder in it. "Petroleum," said Eleanor.

Archie Rowe had an infallible, Levant perception of all the shades of everything that didn't matter. Or did petroleum matter? There were wells here, drills there, claims somewhere other ... the Standard-oil people. She let Eleanor get on with it, while she tried to detach herself from them, by listening in, on her own, to the actual petroleum, in person at her shoulder. What would he say about it?

IT WAS NOT that the voice was so specifically "American," though it was that. It was the quality of the tone, rather than the words or the accent, that seemed to vibrate in a different atmosphere, or in a different *lack* of atmosphere would perhaps be more explicit. They bored into the thick Balkan air like one of his own steam-drills. Steam-drill of his accent, made vacuum about it. Each word fell precisely, with a mechanical tip-tap, like words written on a machine. Almost, visibly, a ribbon ticked in the air between them. Madelon listened-in to this arid, not unpleasant voice that somehow, for all its constructed integrity, spelt destruction. It destroyed this thick air, laden with cross-currents and counter-currents of diplomatic suavity, like a truck piled high with dynamite, veering suddenly into a *mardi-gras* carnival. Respecting it, Madelon yet turned with a new vision to the almond-eyed Levant who might, with all his apparent futility, be something true-Persian, out of an art collection. With all his dreary, rather oiled Levant-like stupidity, there was a suggestion, as of a garden; minute, flat roses twined over a trellis, his non-communicable eyes looked inward. Spice-jasmine might not exactly express anything about him. It was a sensation, maybe a false sensation, but spare me from the steam-drill. I'd rather rot with Omar.

I know this rotting with Omar is quite wrong and Athens is the last place to say it, but spare me from the steam-drill. Nevertheless, she continued to follow the tick-tick in the air, with a sort of fascination of desperation. No wonder the world fears this hundred-percent American; we must be loyal to it. It deflates Archie Rowe, for one thing, and values the studied negligence and would-be aristocratic insolence of his expensively acquired manner, at its worth. It manages to put in its place, the not unmusical low drawl, that is the head of the British school of Athens, speaking French, with that explicit sort of accent, to the sallow complexioned Levant, who might be Persian. Persians and Greeks. The petroleum-king said nothing actively destructive, but what he said demolished everything. No *léger-de-main* of the unconscious or sheer conscious ingenuity, could really, ever (could it?) link Sparta up with oil-wells and the Hellespont with steam-drills? Archie was speaking of these same things, but in a slightly superior manner now, to Eleanor. Archie would consider it beneath his dignity to refer to Xerxes, Thucydides or what not; he ignored the surface values of antiquity. Not so the petroleum magnate. He peppered his discourse with them. Yet his phrases suggested a thumbed text-book, rather than reality, either spiritual or economic. He was discussing an excursion with the secretary, whose slightly weary intonation vaguely suggested Boston. Delphi, he was explaining, was quite out of the question, the road was broken, or flooded or taken over by brigands. Anyhow, they couldn't get to Delphi. He might charter some sort of tramp to take them to Aegina. She should see Eleusis … Marathon … a tablet set up to the thousand slain at Thermopolae, or was it at Château Therry?

Xerxes – Salamas – Woodrow Wilson – the Ulysses-bow of the last Geneva conference – the Achilles heel of something or somebody or other – a dump of supplies, left by a battleship that hadn't managed to get to Constantinople – this was all so much old iron, scrap-iron, to be disposed of. But not to be annihilated just like that, dynamited to nothing; O, no! There were waste products to be utilized, the very thoughts, one felt, of Socrates still gave off their utilitarian by-product. The slender, intellectualized fingers were manipulating, well in anticipation of dessert, the long, slender cigar. He was already waiting for his cigar. For a moment, that pair of apparently ill-assorted Americans, who yet vibrated to something (for all her tenderly, weary Boston manner) in com-mon, seemed more astonishing than any mere flagrant white Russians, escaping by way of a black sea, from a red peril. The white Russians were apparently doomed. How long would they hold out? Probably just as long as they could accrue credit, or attain merit, from the diamonds.

She had got it down to dollars and diamonds. (One must hold on to something.) The mid-West by way of Wall Street voice, ruled lines on paper, neat columns of debit and loss and fractional margins. Say one, nine, two, O, and link it up to something. Anything, everything else here, fluttered in and out of the dimensions, in and out of history, destroyed the most simple time-values, brought pre-war into some perspective but by way of things forgotten or relegated to an attic, with old copies of Floradora. The old-copy-book with lines, ruled in precise fours, and the thumbed score of Floradora were resurrected here, and here, of all places. History repeated itself in white-Russian coiffures, out of a smart showcase of the late nineties. Have we come to Athens for this?

Dollars and diamonds, at least, punctuated all this; the only feasible and solid points of reality were, yet, the most unreal. The white Russians depended on that most mystical value, a value set by some Levant merchant on two diamonds, on their lives exactly. Wall Street might totter, at any moment, like a too-high wall of bricks, come tumbling down and Liberty fall, with a splash, to rust in the north river. Liberty? Wasn't that just the thing that had held the show together? *Acropole et Angleterre*, she read again under her breath, pretending to scan the menu. But that combination was impossible.

Not so impossible. Wasn't there Lord Byron by the Zappeon Garden, wasn't there Timon of Athens … Maid of Athens … why not? There was no tracking down reality, through poetry, or was it the Prophilia? I've not had more than two glasses. Archie tilts the bottle toward me as I finger the stem of my glass, an almost empty crystal goblet in which I might see anything. Hold on to some reality. What then, is reality? Diamonds? Petroleum? White wine, certainly, with a name, *Prophilia*. She wanted to ask Archie Rowe about the other wines here. But as he was still outlining, in a slightly self-deprecatory manner, pronunciation of modern Greek for Eleanor, she let her mind slide off this suave, too-subtle layer and slip back to the uncompromisingly pitched voice that was now holding forth to the secretary, likewise on Greek etymology. His was more practical, explicit; it applied equally to Woodrow Wilson and to Pericles. Autocracy, he was explaining to the slightly (one felt) supercilious secretary, was rule of the few, democracy (ah, there we are) of the many. There was plutocracy as well (he must know all about that), demos, he said was their state, a deme. O, the United States of Pericles, yes certainly. It was a new light on that past. Demos, a deme, our state, the English county, or the French province (he knows everything). Archie was now holding forth, rather more from the autocratic level, on a little "do" at Oxford. How long would Eleanor conceal the barb that was on the verge of being let fly? Madelon would have been interested in hearing Archie Rowe's paternal grandfather's history, an Englishman of the Gladstone and the seven-isles' tradition. Archie would probably consider it "not done" to be too serious about the old Ionian controversy. Madelon would be sure to approach the subject from exactly the wrong angle. She was tired of the arid vibration of the magnate. Did one come here to Athens to learn facts, with a midwest accent, from the back of the dictionary, over Greek white wine? How could she reach Archie, before Eleanor let her barb fly? If she said something definitely to do with nineteen-twenty, she might make a *lié*. She said, *lié, liaison, heptanésos*.

She breathed *heptanésos,* under her breath, no use saying it out aloud. It meant the seven islands, but she didn't dare pronounce it. She deliberately shut out the arid mid-west voice that went on talking about democracy. She thought, democracy, a deme, daemon, diamond. She thanked Archie Rowe, yes a drop more, but (archly) no more – how exactly did you pronounce it? *Prophilia,* the Greek word looked so exciting, written like that, in Greek letters, on the bottle. He said she was quaint, managing, curiously, to insert a *w* between the syllables, breaking up the word in syllables and managing (how did he do it?) to insinuate his overworked lisping *w* somewhere. He asked them if they had any other special preference for Greek wine, he himself preferred French always, the implication being that they had made a social blunder, or not? She answered, anyway, with no hesitation, exalted by the sound and delight of it, *Mavrodaphne.* She had no idea of what it was like, she said, had only seen the word printed, and the look of it made her quite drunk. "O, old *'daphne,"* he dismissed it.

But now they were on the subject of grapes, couldn't he talk about them? She wanted to ask him about their different vineyards, about red, black and white grapes, some sort of dwarf-grape she had heard mentioned somewhere, that someone said was not the usual currant. Grapes ripened specifically flavoured, she had been told, on the rock-slopes of Achaea, and wasn't that (hadn't he told them earlier) his nome? Demos, a deme, nomos, a state or wasn't it? There were the white mulberry trees and black. Did they make wine from the berries? Silk worms? These were the things that mattered. But Archie Rowe would go on impressing himself and the neighbouring tables, about somebody-or-other at Oxford who had been sent down, or sent up (did they know him?) not turning his slant fish eyes, but drawing their attention, by a flutter of an eyebrow, to another excellency or other who had entered. The wife of the American military attaché was by far the best dressed woman in the room. She wore a bundle of violets, at her waist. She sat a little too self-consciously erect, "quaint," as Archie would have put it, as her arm bent awkwardly to the suave formality, as that excellency bent to brush her fingers. She was young, happy, pretty, no doubt superlatively tactful, but she creaked, just a little, in her social joints.

SOMEONE, not visible, the other side of the attaché, was saying in another near-Boston voice (another petroleum secretary?) that they were all like that, tiresome, and she was sure that Allie shouldn't be hurt about it. Would her mother please tell Allie (dear child) that they were all like that? Why shouldn't she do a little digging? Poor little thing, it showed a suitable interest, didn't it? And with that pathetic little pen knife, saved over, so touching, from her school pencil box, at home. That really was the last touch. Who was it had pounced on her? And from what excavation trench, exactly? She'd have something to say to them (tell Allie) … This famous Allie was no doubt the leggy child she had brushed against, on the stairs, taking two at a time, gallantly, till she saw some grown-up coming. Allie was now, apparently, upstairs, sleeping.

One looked through one eye of Archie Rowe and out of the other. He had two eyes, for a Chelsea art-ball, painted over a sallow, pink, English-Levant face. His mother drew far away. One could not visualize a pure Greek mother for this. She lived at Patras. They must stop at Patras, he said, on their way up the Corinthian Gulf. He wanted them to see all the "beawty spots," Corfu certainly. They awaited, while a bodiless, pseudo-French confection, of sorts, was shoved between their shoulders.

The young wife of the American military attaché was obviously very popular. The clear hyacinth-pink and wedgewood-blue and primrose-yellow of the gowns she had worn, with suitable accessories, these three nights to dinner, made Madelon think of the paper-dolls she had cut out as a child, with a bouquet or a parasol or a basket to match each individual costume. It was as if these notable frocks were flimsy things to dress a doll in. The fabulous Russian had only one frock obviously. The clothes of the English group were weathered and a bit old-fashioned, apparently, by choice. The paper-doll brought the backs of coloured magazines into focus. Who would have expected that here? Wasn't it enough to cope with history in its magnified and heroic dimensions, without bringing in an apple-blossom paper doll, who could never have been Marie Antoinette? People, here, were all out of art-collections. Why this doll?

Even Archie here, for instance, as he turned the other fish-side, in possible recognition of yet another "celeb-wity," was almost out of an Egyptian room, albeit in a provincial and not very good collection. He was second-rate but authentic. His dinner jacket was too perfect. His hands were podgy but sensitive, he was not, in the least, what he most affected, English. There was, now, the tuning-up of an orchestra – did Archie say, Hungarian? – from a gallery. Music lifted the floor and the tables with it, to a blue danube period waltz. They were whirled high and dropped, as down the shaft of a lift, by the whirlwind bow of the leader, who shook dark hair forward, to greet applause, over a balcony. It was only the preliminary bars, to show what they could do. Now he began in earnest.

They sometimes cleared the tables, Rowe said, toward midnight, did Miss Eddington dance? Eleanor shot a shocked "certainly not" at Archie, who retired, like a turtle, into his dinner-jacket. There was a pronounced flutter of heightened conversation, as they drew near coffee. Would they like it in the lounge? Eleanor snapped "no" to him. It was all going to be too difficult with Eleanor.

A SINGLE VIOLIN cut a swallow-wing pattern through the air, and she would be transposted with it, if she were not careful. Even to think "*heptanésos*, seven-isles," was too much. She could not yet afford to try her own wings, float above this heavy laden atmosphere, herself hover above clouds of cigarette-smoke – incense? – toward this near sky. Perhaps they were right to shut out what was so real.

There was a slice of that Turkish delight that Rowe had been talking about on the edge of a small plate. A tiny coffee cup held too-black coffee, but she ought by now – after all of three days – to be used to it. She looked at the semi-transparent slab of thick sweet, powdered with soft sugar. "Is this that honey-and-sesame *loukoumi* you spoke of," she asked Rowe, though it couldn't possibly be anything else, "do have one of my cigarettes," managing a little stage-business, on the side, for Eleanor was being tiresome. Obviously, Eleanor wanted Archie Rowe to go home, but obviously, he couldn't do that quite yet. "Do they put dope in these things?" What now, had she said to him? The honey-and-sesame tasted, to the tongue, like soothing syrup or a cough drop, it was strangely aromatic, in an unknown dimension. It was Keats – what was it – all that mixture of syrup-steeped fruits and peel and candied citron. It was things in jars, on a shelf, in an old-fashioned country store; opium? Poppy-seed. The room went round and with it, the Russian diamonds. It's getting too hot here.

It was no hotter than it had been. Outside lay a street lined with fern-shaped trees that dropped red berries. Across the street, shallow steps led down into a garden, a winter square, where already a few orange trees promised an early blossom. Under smoke and silver olives, two bronze deer stood alert. She had walked that morning in the garden of the king, *kepos basilikos*, they called it. She had hesitated before entrances to little churches that were set, squat, like bee hives, facing the newer thoroughfare. She had smelt that invidious incense that yet did not draw her in, to worship. She had turned off the market, into the street of Pan, to face three such squat churches, Soter, Stephen and Simon, was it? Impressions mellowed by time, yet remained distinct. Now she was losing something. She was beginning to sag toward Lethe; where there was so much to remember, why not forget? Or was it the hint, back of her mind, of poppies?

She must say something. The only thing that vied, in clarity, with debit and credit, and the idea of numbers ruled on paper, was a flight of silver, that was yet a violin that, with all its exaggerated and emotionally timed rise and fall, swept over their heads, out to the bluer aether. With it, as she watched it, were those sharply defined impressions of columns, cut against blue, against violet, against deep violet, against purple, as the sun sank beyond Lycabettos. Lycabettos rose like a ship about to set sail, Hymettus rested like a ship in harbour. Only the Acropolis remained static, itself a harbour, an island above a city, a city set on a hill, an idea that, in all its eternal and remote dimension, still cut patterns in the race mind, the human consciousness, now murky with din and battle, as that violin's rhythm and sway, cut pattern across fumes of countless cigarettes, the dreary reiteration of a thousand diplomats. She must hold on a little longer.

Rowe was, at last, trying to placate Eleanor, frankly, with comparative Greek pronunciations. O, but keep him, keep him away from Homer. Why should I keep him away from Homer? Why not listen to what he may say? O, don't, don't listen to Archie Rowe making the right comparisons, soothing down the intensity of the classics, devitalising, as he had been expensively taught to do, his mother's racial heritage. Keep Archie Rowe off this, at any price. Say anything. She found herself pronouncing in a rapt voice – he will think I am quite mad, – "Ah, the Acropolis." Now what would she do about it? There was nothing to do about it but keep on.

Her words fluttered into the thing they had avoided all that evening. She had broken a taboo, it was not "done" to talk about Ionian columns against violet, in Athens, in nineteen-twenty. She listened to the violin, lost its silver pattern, say something. Eleanor would not help her, was delighted that she was caught. A net drew over her mood, the silver flash of her own wit must save her. But her words fell, too late, between them, annihilated diplomacies, space, time and distance, "It's smaller than anyone could think. It's smaller and colder. It's frozen. It's alive. It's more alive than anything living to-day. It's far and cold, like a flower frozen under white ice. It is white ice, and white fire. It has never been ruined, for it has never been built. It's in a state of building." Archie Rowe was gazing at her, as if pointedly, by inference, to avoid what must be evident. This lady wasn't used to Greek wine, even their light *Prophilia* went to her head, or was she quite mad? "It's like a flower seen frozen in a crystal. It's even more luminous than anything, anyone yet saw; someone dreamed it … in a crystal."

Nothing mattered, now that she had said this. She was burning with that fanatic fervour that leads eccentric, middle-aged derelicts to stand up, on a tub at Hyde Park Corner, and hold forth about the millennium. She was holding forth and she didn't care who saw it. Then she remembered Eleanor. Archie Rowe is her guest, I am the guest of Eleanor. Now, how could she retrieve it? Anything was better than this, this fervour about the Parthenon in Athens. She leaned over swiftly, in a moment annihilated her social blunder by one, only a shade less flagrant, yet still permissible. She actually whispered, "*those diamonds.*"

He looked at her, as if he hadn't seen her, then as if he saw her. He didn't say anything, there was nothing to say. Of course, he had chapter and verse up his sleeve, but he wouldn't divulge the secret. Mrs. – ah – Thorpe, wasn't (he was now quite certain) – ah – quite one of us. He turned to Eleanor.

But now she was free.

MADELON LOOKED at the girl frankly, but now saw her as something, again, different. But what she saw her as she could not yet say. Was the Russian woman doomed, by some law deeper than the social law of gossips and of diplomats? Were rigorous laws functioning here, laws far older than the Norman Conqueror, the authentic county inheritance of the head of the British school, at work here? Was there some vein of mystery, some occult knowledge that they all shared? Was mid-west right to ignore Salamis, except as a stepping-stone to oil wells, and was little Allie (upstairs sleeping) protected and forewarned, when some authorised academic snob purloined her pen-knife from her? Could they, even today, dig too deep? Was it wise to penetrate below a surface that the British school so carefully kept in its place, that an opera-bouffe royal family had the wit and courage to ignore, that Archie Rowe, with a mother from Achaea, went to Oxford expensively to forget? They should have ordered French wine, certainly, *Bordeaux; Hock* even.

Last night, the night before, after a three weeks' broken and exciting voyage, had been stepping stones (Salamis, to oil wells) to this night. Tonight was different, tonight she was whirled into the whirlpool in a backwater, the scum of little tables was lifted high, they were all flung out and back into unpredictable dimensions. Was it merely the *Prophilia?* Did poppy juice distil all this, from a sugar-sweet, sugar-coated bit of sticky sweetmeat? Black coffee took off the taste of sugar-coated sugar, but something lingered, a suspicion, a taste in another direction. O no, it wasn't opium, Archie had laughed at them. What was it, if it wasn't opium?

The walls lifted and fell to the tune of a blue-danube epoch, *Mavrodaphne* was a word to beware, even *Prophilia* might conjure, who knows what from the floor. Who knows what might rise, like a ball-room Mephistopheles out of this floor? Here, anything might happen. The voices of the Americans who were departing in a cluster, cut its zip-pattern into the blue danube. The British school was speaking English casually now, to an acquaintance who had risen to join his table. Waiters, less astutely, balanced trays and swept crumbs off tables, less ostentatiously. There was a pause, like a breath drawn. Diamonds.

It was all there. A secret that she hadn't striven to solve, that she had dismissed as unworthy of solution, the way they began to draw things, in cut-off triangles and the way they superimposed things, in the new painting. In London, that hadn't come true, quite to her, but she saw now, what the eccentric new art sought for. She wanted to shout to Eleanor, Eleanor Eddington, E.E. or Edd as she had learned to call her; she wanted to snatch the core of herself out of Madelon Thorpe, Madd as Eleanor called her, she wanted something, unrelated to time, related to infinity, to communicate with something unrelated to time, related to infinity. Make that correspondence and nothing else matters, you may dismiss Archie

Rowe and the head waiter and the breakfast butler upstairs (who would mistake her for Eleanor) in a breath. You related time-out-of-time, to time-in-time and you get snatches of each, in bits of jagged-off triangles. In your mind you have a sort of tube, like their nursery kaleidoscope, all the colours are there, violet, violets of Hymettus, ultra-violet and sea-purple; you say *Mavrodaphne* and you get drunk, she had told Archie, like that. *Prophilia* was something different. It was the sharp edge of a cut-off triangle that must be the one facet of that diamond. That must be each facet of a diamond that was a new way of thinking. Everything dissolved in the chemistry of this post-war, Balkan dining-room, in the *Hotel Acropole et Angleterre,* but this thing. A new way of looking at things....

Don't look at the diamond. Eleanor is shuffling her feet and I'll have to wait till Rowe, tediously, takes leave before, upstairs, I can burst into this new layer, this new discovery, before I can tell Edd, or E.E., as I have learned to call her, how she can paint pictures like that. This is the new music. Everything seems unrelated yet diametrically related, as you slant one facet of a diamond into another set of values.

PONTIKONISI
(MOUSE ISLAND)

I DON'T KNOW what it's about but I have found a formula, she said. Mouse Island lay flat on the green water, like a raft. Someone had unfolded a Hansel and Gretel peak-roof out of the wrong box. One toy-tree stood in a tub. Door and window were marked in nursery-stencil. If you fold up Hansel and Gretel, out of the wrong Blue Bird set, you should unroll paste-board pillars. It would come right.

The Ionian Sea was green glass from a night-club roof, lit all round the sides with white electricity. From their paste-board crag, they looked down through the roof onto wavering streamers and green fronds. Harps out of the water and the buttocks of a sea-centaur would make it rightly Böcklen. People like that came here, before they went to Capri. Ana-Capri and the Barbarossa turrets were so much purple-chalk on grey cardboard, compared with this thing. This was much worse than Capri. Capri deluded no-one into thinking it was other than delusion. This deluded one into the frigid heart of a cameo, one turned round and, fly-in-amber, spoiled the contour. The whole thing was hacked out with an ice-pick.

No one had taught her to think like that but she thought under her thought: it's moss-agate, it's a sort of Poe-Baudelaire dope-dream frozen. People must have thought this way or a fly under a purple crocus. This purple was to Capri-bloom, fire through iris-petal, compared to blue chalk. But this was not what she thought. She remembered Capri as a digression. Capri was true-siren island but Odysseus swept past that. His ship was rock, Pontikonisi, in this bay.

Madelon must flick back pages of a Baedeker, to find out whether Pontikonisi or the other-island was really that ship. The other-island was meticulously etched, it had spared one tree only of the Noah's Ark trees for Pontikonisi. Pontikonisi's one tree seemed to make itself important in a tub. The trees on the other-island belonged with the island. You could roll the thing up, a spiky untrimmed Robinson Crusoe's island out of still another of the toy-theatre sets. The things were to be swept up, put in their separate boxes; which? Man was important, woman was important, but a boy-child was more apt at jack-the-giant-killing. She thought now of Paul Hampton's army boot as filling up the canvas. It would descend with giant latches, like door-hinges on a door, and separate spikes in the soles. She thought of Paul Hampton, terrible with banners, then crouched over a drawing-board. She rebelled against Dora out of Dickens holding pencils. She offered cast-iron exterior to cover, if possible, the suppressed Victorian sentiment. She would like to wear crinoline, watch Paul Hampton's swift hand. They sometimes called those trees lead-pencil cypress. The other-island was a porcupine with spiked quills. She would have beaten against Hampton's chest with her fists, let me in, let me in, let me in. Now that she had so terribly dismissed him, she wanted to crawl back like a mouse, live in his shoe.

That man would set his shoes down by the side of his bunk and any woman, passing his cabin to the ladies-only, would go mad. He left his door open of course, and lay there, with his pebble-thick glasses off, ironically in purple. He grinned, not being asleep of course, with eyes closed. The sun, the wind that had gnawed at his tough skin, left indeterminate eye-sockets, so that the un-burnt white on and about his closed lids made ghost-sockets. He was laid-out, ironically smiling, in state; the red ship-blanket with black stripes was death-purple drawn even to his chin. The knees peaked slightly to keep his feet in. The coffin was by that much, too short. She wondered what he did with his glasses, they seemed part of his face, necessities like false teeth. She thought of his face as wounded, gaping, there was something illicit about the alarming candor of those eyes. The eyes seen through the glasses were mini-mized, insignificant. When he jerked them off with that finality, to use the field-glasses or to point some remark at coffee, he seemed, with apt legerdemain, to have flicked back a curtain. The show was spread out, gilt ladders and mirrors, white rabbits in top hats, a flight of doves, a disappearing woman in a cabinet, that last, herself. She saw herself back of the formality of his manner, in Felican Rops black gloves. She would wear black period gloves, shoes cut like gloves. Her legs would make angle with the floor, points of the an-gle stressed with black-shoe marks. Her body would break a pencil line, white, black, white, her arms would stretch to a T-square. Was she angles and triangles in his mind? She must have made a mark there. Or she was a living canker, curled there, loving? She thought of loving in terms of a worm, eating flesh like chestnuts.

FIZZ SAT ON her feet and promised to bring her coffee. Madelon felt for the side of that ship-bunk and found it was the bed. Salt wind should have been blowing on her from the right, she had the port-hole top-berth. Fizz would sit alert and beat at her through the bunk slats. Fizz was awkward on ship. She would tilt the bed now, stretched over the end rail, doing a trapeze turn. She wore the green pyjamas, she lurched forward as if her hair really pulled her down. It was an untidy sheen, tied with a frayed ribbon. Fizz was Fleece of Gold, a disproportionate Veronese. She should have been a young reigning English beauty, but was heavy, dropped and bungled things. She disclaimed grace. She butted like a ram and had no sense of levels. She ran up-hill or loped down. She said, "Pallaeokastrizza."

The word buzzed like Pandora-flies let loose out of that box. "Dress – get-up – coffee – we're going – " The words blurred off; heard off, they were vision-like, blurred lense in ears. Ears saw and eyes heard, it was that honey-fragrance of stale locust-blossom, "throw it out – it makes me sick – we shouldn't have brought back that branch of blossom." Fizz would do anything she said, awkwardly, to express herself. A green arm thrust out and removed the jam-jar from the top of the commode. The room was terrible, Madelon saw what it was. Fizz had flung open the window and irregular slats of light showed above dazzling sheet-metal. "Let the shutters down, can't you – " but Fizz had gone. She would have to endure solid sheet-gold and, above it, the other tilted half of unkempt Venetian shutter.

Fizz or Fitz was a starry person, quite suitable but exhausting. Eleanor Fitzroy, Madelon said to herself, to get Fizz in pattern. She was a wicked creature, letting in sun to show waste. There was a black steel engraving above a horse-hair sofa. Rays of light emerged from the retreat from Moscow, or was it Moses, striking hornlight from rock? The wash-stand had a rose jug from one set and a mauve bow-knot basin from another. Fizz had left the jug on the floor last night. Madelon wished that the tooth-mug and the soap-dish hadn't matched either, they belonged to the mauve knots. The china was on the shadow-side, fortunately. It seemed, even through her closed lids, that reflections from porcelain would drive her mad. Her sea-sickness took itself out on land, she was never ill on board. Or was it that break toward re-birth, artificial psychic caesarian, America-Europe, beginning to tell now? The place where the graft was, rubbed raw. She hadn't felt it till this letting go London, where her graft-bandages still were. She said Hampton, Paul Hampton to get her rock. Hampton, powerful, dark-magnet, had re-assembled her bits. He had understood when she said, "I am shot to bits."

There was no such ship certainly under the boards they stood on. Cables, rails, wireless station, a compass and a triangular peak at the prow, made for a draped girl to stand on, don't make a boat. That year, of course, had no existence. All surplus energy was used up, to persuade oneself simply, that this was. By that, she was so much richer. In accepting her disintegration plus her potential-ity, Eleanor Fitzroy predicted a new continent. Madelon hadn't known how land-locked she was till she stood on that deck. Eng-land dropped down the Thames like a black stone. Was England ever anything so stolid as a stone? Madelon thought, it's a black sponge, it's become black, it's soaked up so much. It seemed the tip of that foggy island was the feeler of one of those ink-octopus crea-tures, that claws out to the world, takes and squeezes dry and turns everything to poison. It was her immediate problem. When she turned from that boat rail, blind with a sort of final repudiation … she had taken it all back. Hampton stood watching with her. He said, "I was in Jerusalem … demobbed, came back to get my pa-pers." He had got some sort of papers, still wore his old army boots, he had been in Arabia and India. That much for octopus-England; you met this other on ships.

She had said, "is there any life for us," before she knew his name. Fizz came in and banged down the tray.

Madelon sat up with the pillows at her back and her line of vision altered so that she saw the tops of the orange-trees. They ran almost flat like clipped box and blossom was thick this year. Rosettes of flowers were out of a Botticelli sequence. "I couldn't help it," Fizz said, "she would put that on your tray." Madelon was thinking that the flowers were almost too symmetrical on the box-level floor of those trees. She saw that the waitress had again propped one of those intolerable sprays of orange-blossom by her bread.

If she let her head fall back, slide back from the support of that bed-rail under her pillow, she thought she would slide out; it was fainting into some sort of numbness. Why wouldn't they let her go? When she wanted to slide right down through the mattress into the pit-black of annihilation, things happened. She said, "pour out my coffee, can't you, Fizz," and had to risk Fizz ruining her sheets. Fizz managed it. The fluid in her throat shot back life. "They've got it hot this time – we must ask her what her name is," Madelon said, though she knew they couldn't correlate the syllables when that woman, they called Medea, did speak. The hotel servant for the most part, and the man who drove them round the island, spoke Italian. Any Greek word had to be spelt out here in terms of super-imposed civilization, Turkish or Armenian.

Fizz sat on the bed, dressed. She poured useful articles out of a bag and made calculations with a silver pencil. "Who didn't we tip last week?" "Don't do Medea's today, she'll think it's for these flowers." Madelon broke bread, over stimulated. She perceived it was neither Moses nor Moscow. "Who is that preposterous person in the gold frame there, with laurels?" Fizz said, "a drachma is a lire, is a franc, isn't quite a shilling – isn't it?" "Don't know. I can't calculate dollars even, nor cents." Money seemed to her to be seen in museum-cases, numismatic, she believed the word was, collections, a red Indian penny carefully mounted and the reverse side. She thought of money in terms of numismatics, for Fizz had relieved her of that counting and re-considering, two-and-six is more than fifty cents, for so long; something in her head, along with the other things in her head, felt unweighted. She had, she supposed, thrown out too much ballast, and even thinking of coins, the thought of Hampton and Spanish silver slipped into his palm, for that cab. Fizz must have slipped it in my pocket, she does sometimes, when we left the tender at Gib. She said, you can calculate it out on the boat if you're so trivial, but it isn't even mine, it's Fizz's. They walked up the hill. The others were waiting in the courtyard of the Reina Christina. The dining room was a grey tunnel, and Spanish boys in flannels drifted about and English boys from the garrison. There was no churning of that ship-cable and there wasn't any music.

The noise of the silence beat about her ears in the dining room of the Reina Christina, at Algeciras, like grey wings.

THE SENSATION of his nearness went through her like white flowers. Fizz said when she took the trip last time, before the war, they had stopped at the Achileion, did she want to see it, if she felt tired, they could put off Pallaeokastrizza, see the Achilleion gardens. She had said no, she didn't want to stop. If the two horses stopped, turned round, and the jog-jog of their stopping pulled up in dust, the electric-white, the presence of Paul Hampton would pass from her. They were jogging in a monotonous delirium toward the Potano; respective holy mountains cut card-board blue

35

and green peaks into a near-blue porcelain heaven. Santi Deca and Kyriaké might or might not be those peaks; they must have passed Santi Deca; but that was the other time at Canone, looking down on water, Mouse Island and Santi Deca and Kyriaké. Madelon didn't think her mind could mop up any more sensations. If the two horses stopped their jog-jog now, they would walk between box hedges from Versailles and a poet would scrutinize them from an alcove. That, she believed, was Heine. Eleanor had ironically outlined the attractions of the late Kaiser's palace, eucalyptus, palm, magnolia and aloe, and terraces over the sea, graded for the Elizabeth of Austria, but not for the late Kaiser would she step out into anybody's scenery. This wasn't the Kaiser's scenery nor Isadora Duncan's. She herself had made it, she and a silver-platinum that followed or fled, that was platinum white of orange-blossom that was Paul Hampton. She would jog-jog forward into that search-light.

If it came to Italian she could say what do they call it, and she asked Makkas what the hedge was. He said agave or something she inferred was that, anyway she said to Fizz that sort of cactus that they have in Sicily. The road was lined with dusty opuntia cactus, prickly pear or Indian apple with a gash now and again into a garden where callas would group, in the Capri manner, in a cool corner round a wine-jar. The road opened by live arms of a Marconi station, which excited Makkas back into Greek, and a dry river. Further inland, it wound through hedges of the wild-quince in bloom. The quince, she remembered, was called valonia on Pylos, and they had had that quince-preserve, with black olives, pimento-peppered omelette and black coffee. Paul Hampton had been informative and she had laughed. He had wanted to come with them. Currants, olive-oil and soap, she had intoned ironically, are the chief exports from Zante, oranges, lemons and flowers.

Hagia Metamorphosis is Transfiguration, she told Fizz.

THE MONKS AT Palaeokastrizza left them alone. Makkas pointed frantically to the wall door, they could go in there. They dropped down, however, to a steam-rolled plaque of gold sand, the monastery garden could wait. Sand lay hammered and beaten, sun beat half to gold, the shadow was unconvincingly too black. They sat near the edge of shadow, half under a boat. The boat had no name, but Hagia Metamorphosis could send Paul Hampton to them.

They would select a share of the white chicken, buttered white rolls and an egg for Makkas. He waited above with the horses, engaged in some mysterious business with the harness. He was always surprised, in an operatic Verdi manner, when they took him rolls, the egg, half of the white-wine, cheese, and some fruit. He would sit down a little apart, propped up against an olive, his hat over his eyes. Madelon remembered the salt, you better take him some salt. The sun would stand still. The cliffs to the right of this curve of the Bay of Liapades, were honeycombed, crumbling with white earth. The sea was level as glass, the strip of sand they sat on curved slightly upward like a shallow bowl. The usual olives tangled grey with silver and dull jade and aubergine. Madelon pushed aside her hotel napkin with egg-shells and spilt salt.

She would drop her head back into the shadow, her palms must turn black. As she stretched out palms, crucified to sunlight, her thought-under-her-thought informed her of Emmaus. Even when they brought sticks and dry olive leaves to build a fire, by just this boat, they didn't at first recognize him. If he could strip Hampton of Hampton, who shouldn't he galvanize the phantom into reality?

37

She found afterwards, in the storm when she had talked to Hampton, that Hampton had been below deck. It couldn't be possible for Hampton to project himself or perhaps he had done. If she had known the first rules of the game, she would have asked him. But of course, when she found out that it was a game, it was too late. If his lovers didn't know him on the Emmaus road, how could she know him, until after Paul Hampton had left? She had no intention of confusing Paul Hampton himself with the galvanized projection.

Eleanor had said certainly, it seemed feasible. She said, "Fizz do you mind if I sleep?" The sun would beat and beat and beat, which way was the shadow going? Madelon might say, if the sun rode upward, lifting the black shadow from her face, her truth was truth. But she couldn't, at the moment, risk too facile oracle. "Throw me the cigarettes, please Fizz." She sat up, a fly buzzed heavily towards the other napkin and a broken tangerine.

SHE COULDN'T ALLOW herself to go to sleep, it would be illicit, like taking dope or something. Her nerves were shot to bits, but she must stay awake sometimes. She would wake in the night to ascertain where she was. She could run her fingers over Pennsylvania grave-stones, say, these are my people, this is my name. She hadn't wanted to see any of them, barring torpedo-crossings, even if the London Foreign Office had given her a passport. It was fantastic the way they had dropped out, only Rag, in France, this side.

Her thought over her thought had the cool surface intention of a torpedo, certainly. She didn't want to see any of them, really hadn't cared when she learnt how Rag went. Their names were compounded with the other-dead Electras and Agemmemnons. A thing is dead, it's dead, there's no time that side. Hampton had had somewhat her own idea of no-time. He had been in the East anyway. She couldn't allow any of them to come into consciousness any more than she could have allowed her crinoline-incarnation to dwell on the thought of Paul Hampton, responsible with a drawing board.

She recognized this as being what Fizz in the then new psycho-analytical jargon would have termed a suppression. She had said, Oh cut out old p. a., (as they called it) to Fizz. But P. A. became capitalized, it was comforting to know nowadays there were specialists in the thought-under-the-thought. Some day when she had time, she would find out why she had put the weights on the thought to keep it down that way. She had her formula, she was platinum sheet-metal over jelly-fish. The inside could get out that way, only when the top was broken. It was the transcendentalist inside that had met Hampton in the storm on deck, when Paul Hampton was downstairs in the smoking-room.

SMOKE WREATHED UPWARD from a half-cigarette and she wondered how she could mark time longer. She would have to break silence, bring her thought back. There were a handful of shells at her elbow, she and Rag had quarreled about the tiny sand-forms, he had said she could have the fish anyway, it looked like a cake-tin. He had let her have the fish though he wanted it himself and had had to colourate his unselfishness so it would look as if he were just as happy with the oak-leaf. They had always tossed a coin to find who would choose first, they went solemnly through sets of animals, sets of sand-toys, sets of paper soldiers. Heads you win, tails I lose. She was bound to lose anyway: Paul Hampton. It would have to happen that way. The thought-under-the-thought would compel her to lose the thing. She couldn't be Paul Hampton's lover because the thought-under-the-thought had jerked back to the suppression. She hadn't really cared when Rag went. The reason was that Rag and his like had never gone west. There was no west to go to. Paul Hampton might have been Raglain. Only Hampton didn't have to be told things. His chosen confederate on the boat was the little jockey on his way out to Egypt to some Pasha Ali Achmed or other's stables. Paul Hampton's eyes met hers through the tennis-tournament platitudes of the Alexandrine lady-leader of the colony. She was too tired to care, and exterminated with her marriage.

Of course, she had never really married anybody, loving Raglain too much.

SHE STOOD UP on legs that wouldn't hold her any longer. Let's stagger back to that cab, don't let's see Saint Angelo nor the garden.

NARTHEX

γαρθηξ: wand carried by initiates ... original plant-stalk by means
of which Prometheus brought fire from heaven.

1

AEONS BRUSHED THROUGH her and made a sort of buzzing ... which is ridiculous. She looked up into parallelogram
and straight geometric static upright parallels upholding myriad
geometric caryatids; the straight parallels of ceilings, roofs above
ceilings, mapped out with T-square, with ruler for king and doge
and emperor. Saint Mark's Square stretched side-wise, parallel to
Saint Mark's Square stretched side-wise and Saint Mark's Square
at her back was perpendicular to Saint Mark's Square at her left,
to Saint Mark's Square at her right. Before her, set just there as
if carefully placed by some careful child, was Saint Mark's. Saint
Mark's, now she faced the thing, was a heap of child blocks and
child stone-blocks and child box of building-blocks on obvious
child stone arches. Set on top of Saint Mark's was an assortment
of odd things pulled off the Christmas tree, oddments discarded
as not neat enough, not shiny enough for "next year." Domes, half
balls, Christmas-tree balls depleted of bright Christmas-tree gold
and half Christmas-tree balls were set carefully so as not to show
where and how some careless child had cracked them. Along the
front of the preposterous edifice were cones, also tarnished, of
prickly undefined ornaments, undefined, not fitting in with the

neatness and the artifice that had invented just that box of building blocks with all its elaboration on the set convention. "Saint Mark's Cathedral is a sort of Christmas-tree sort of church, built up to be set under the tree, a sort of ten-cent store sort of cathedral" was the formula for Gareth.

Saint Mark's was that and wasn't that. The formula must do for Gareth. Gareth for some unprecedented reason had taken a dislike to Venice. Well, not quite unprecedented – Raymonde had said she would meet Gareth in Venice (and Daniel) in order to go on … Athens half-formulated, to take a boat … spring cruise, summer cruise, it was all unformulated. Saying "yes, I'll meet you in Venice" had meant just no thing, just how nice to have an excuse to leave one's work and tiny pied-a-terre at d'y Vaud and the rather sterile Alpine winter behind one and the still more sterile memory of last London summer, for … Italy. Mind blurred with thinking, too much work, things half-finished and only just begun, Raymonde had said "Gareth I'll come with you." She hadn't taken into account that X thing, that just wasn't but so theoretically might have been, Daniel. The X thing wasn't Daniel. It was Venice.

"Saint Mark's Cathedral is a sort of Christmas-tree sort of church" … Raymonde went on mechanically putting the thing into mechanical destructive thought, into mechanical destructive language so that Gareth, sitting stiff and upright in the little tin chair of Florian's, should get no remotest inkling of what the thing meant (in all its connotations) now, to Raymonde. "Saint Mark's Square *is* Saint Mark's Square, the thing *is* Saint Mark's Square" was safe anyhow and it was rather surprising to see it here, after years, after wars; the same pigeons, rather plumper, the same people, rather funnier; the same come and go and the same three orchestras playing against each other in the separate niches behind the separate groups of carefully arranged chairs (Florian's carefully differentiated from Aurora and Aurora from whatever the one across the way was) and little tables. All careful and secure as if there had never been wars and revolutions and people coming and going and ships sinking under pillars of sea-salt, swirling, child toys, lead weight, sunk into indefinite leviathan sea water. "There's nothing different about Saint Mark's except the tiny slab" (she had discovered it) "slightly to the right of the middle door-way as you face it" (Raymonde doled out information) "marking the Austrian bomb that didn't go off. Hundreds of bombs dropped mostly in the canals and never killed a pigeon" (common-place now though when that quatro-cento waiter said it, it had sounded quaint; words spoken out of some eighteenth century comedy – these jumbled æons – the right words, maybe it was the stylistic way he had of speaking, *bel paese? caffe nero?* whatever he said became set, styl-ized with his pointed face, bad teeth and cameo-yellow eye-lids) "odd there being so many pigeons" – she must go on talking, with Saint Mark's Square to right, to left, hedging them in safe, holding them in safe; you may walk here, there, said the Venetian, here, there yet no further; geometric, Parthenon-like design, sparcity, purity, tempted yet restrained one. I hold you in, make confines for the spirit, then spill (wine out of formal goblets) my master-colour for you. This, in all strict consciousness, was pure Greek formula … then why should Garry plague them with her "Athens"?

Gareth wanted them to take the boat to Athens. Daniel was making thought-curves and spirals in the air. If one could see the thoughts of Daniel they would be gold, rare gold like marks on lilies … white garden lily, *that* in all consciousness, was notably Athenian but "Athens" as Garry named it became stark, hieratic like some stark unripe pale-greenish lily set against church pews.

Athens wasn't that but Gareth, but Venice was making Athens seem that. Athens as Raymonde visualized it (if Gareth would leave her alone to visualize it simply, not drag her away to go there) was pollen-gold; for all its Parthenon arrangement it smelt of tumbled gardens, not of artificially forced open wax virgin-lilies behind glass in winter garden-suburbs. Gareth would kill Athens for her. How could one leave this just-discovered garden, all this just-apprehended visual sensation, red lilies and small clusters of tiny snake-lilies growing a-symmetrical on tall stems and shades and shades un-named, undifferentiated? Garden reds had to be recalled, little old-fashioned bleeding-heart red, columbine red, things she had forgotten, to bring out, to differentiate red from red. Red brooded (rhododendron and carnation) hatched so to speak new combinations, incredible flamingo beauty. Static mosaic alike and fluid extravagance of drapery flung against polished agate, had reality, took on the oddest attribute; leave the thing at doge-red and be done with it. Cardinal-red, doge-red ... they had their parallels with lilies.

2

INTO THE AIR, climbing up into the air, Daniel's thoughts went in swallow-spirals ... which is ridiculous. Daniel could think T-square and length of parallel lines as well as she could, better than Gareth for all Garry's exquisite pedantry and letters after her ridiculous distinguished little name. Gareth sat ridiculous and exquisite, her small hands struggling with an unfamiliar burnt-brown dog biscuit of an Italian tea-cake, struggling to break it, putting all her intensity into just that thing like a child; as a child one could imagine her struggling with just such naïve intensity with a disproportionate garden rake or a watering-can dragged like a miniature tank across garden gravel. Gareth had a ridiculous way of putting too much dynamic energy into everything, whether it was some ridiculous little thesis signed with her ridiculous little distinguished name, or the collecting of rugs from refractory cab or motor, dealing with the "wrong" people or the "right" people in all the manifold phases of existence. People stared hypnotized into Gareth's hypnotizing gray eyes (she had hypnotized poor Rockway) eyes glazed and too intelligent, becoming blurred with impotence when she reached something to which intelligence has no answer. There was no answer, it was obvious to this thing; to Raymonde sitting too-happy in Saint Mark's Square, to Daniel making spiral-thoughts of swallow curves in sunlight.

Some one said "it's too hot in this corner, shall we move back?" It wasn't Daniel. Some one managed laboured words from some-where but it wasn't Daniel, sitting nordic and elegant, slim width of shoulder, slim, mobile shoulders under grey London cloth and the head bent forward. The nape of exposed neck showed odd unfamiliar, bronze-honey tint, the comment, the seal of the Ve-netian sun on Daniel. Daniel was too white, had been too white. Daniel was a little too perpendicularly erect, had been a little too starkly erect in London. His shoulders drooped now suavely, unself-consciously. He seemed to have let go something. He was Hermes seated at a corridor's far end; heat and affluence of seated Hermes was in the forward bent shoulders of this London Daniel. Daniel newly inheriting his due inheritance (somewhat over-due) of sunlight was no one to have dragged the laboured words from nowhere, "it's too hot here in this corner shall we move back?" It wasn't Garry talking. It obviously was Raymonde.

45

"I'm obviously talking, saying things from nowhere, being no-where, being right here." Time and set cycles of time had shifted for her, years had no bearing on things, had no meaning somehow. Fixed years, revolving on her set track through the fever path of Europe, now meant nothing. Years with Gareth … hyacinth-blue years before the war cloud … separation (Gareth had swerved into activity, those diplomatic dodgings with poor Rockway) then renewal … all meant nothing. Going round like a Tibetan prayer wheel, out of peace, the blue waters of non-entity, into brakish "life," those war years. Now back again into the path of Gareth and another realm of daylight, of sunlight that fell pollen-dust, the edge of sun-eclipse – war-London?

Moving on her somewhat jagged yet none the less firmly pre-established orbit, Raymonde had moved (was it only just last sum-mer?) into the track of Daniel … breaking brioche to the pigeons.

3

THE YEAR MOVED backward as a clock-hand steadily pushed backward, encompassing the whole dial, to last spring. Last spring at this point on the clock face was a curious reversion, moving backward, some point in one's life where one said, "this isn't good enough, I'm getting nothing for it." Just that point a year ago, just a year ago that again was the actual replica of points back and back, moving the dial hand backward years and years, about seven, until one came to Katherine. Katherine made a luminous mark on any dial and to say Katherine brought years back of that into concen-tric circle. Keep the years straight, a sort of picture puzzle, this year and this year and the year I married Ransome. Fredrick Ransome

was out of it ... there was nothing left of them, they were the brakish fever cloud and they were best forgotten. Raymonde Ransome
said, I have held on to Freddie Ransome, on to all they stood for
and the result is that nobody cares, I'm getting old maidish and
preposterous, people are only just worse, the sacrifice was nothing.
Step so to speak (she had so stepped) out of the crimson dial face
of fever stricken Europe and say "I won't be counted in it."

Katherine helped in that instance. People always do help. Say in
the soul I want something, black or white, good or bad, anything
just so you want it enough, up or down and something (with Faust
it was Mephistopheles) will answer. Perversely at that moment
Katherine answered.

One is pinned to the dial that is the overlapping cycle of one's
small years like the centre pin point that holds the clock hands ...
Raymonde looked up and saw Mercaria clock marked just five.
"Soon," she said to herself, thinking back to London, "the little
bells will ding and dang and the bronze Gaul will pop out, like a
bird in a cuckoo clock or the boy or the barometized ballet-skirted
little girl in the barometer. One thing pops out, another thing pops
in. Good, bad," she had said a year ago in London, "I'm fed up."
Ding, ding, and the answering dings that made the just-arrived
tourists in the square turn and stare up and one actually check off
the "sight" in a little note-book. He must have just read "be sure to
note the bronze Gauls on the Mercaria clock tower and the Virgin
crowned with seasons." Germanic back turned toward her, heavy
blocked-in square of back. He must be Swedish. "There's a Swedish
boat in," Raymonde said to Gareth. Ding, ding, I go, you come.
One thing counter-balances another. Years are held to flat years.
We go round and round like clock hands ... Garry was frowning
at her.

Garry had frowned at her in London, frowned at Mordant. "Well, I'm tired of writing." Garry would always frown, a sort of steel blue recorder of her conscience, the sort of needle to her intellectual compass, the thing that Garry was pointed true ... follow your own achievement. Garry couldn't know, odd dissociated half relationship with Rockway (Gareth divorced Rockway) emotion and all its tangled connotations. Garry moved in one cycle, had just one dial to go by. The dial of Garry's achievement was out of all time cycles. It was simply the needle of a compass. Garry didn't understand emotion and all its overlayers, the seasons so to speak, marked in zodiacal symbol like those seasons now part of a sort of coronal to the madonna. The Mercaria clock with its barbarians, the two bronze Gauls posed on the clock tower, were fit symbol of her own life. Love seated, so to speak, that blue garmented love-mother with time ticking away above it.

The sun fell warm on their somewhat London shoulders. London had meant spelt achievement and now London was a faded dial face, a handless clock, figureless, without meaning. O somewhat still with meaning. Wasn't London symbolized at this moment to her by just such sort of somewhat crude carved figures? The two bronze barbarians, the two Gauls posed for some reason surely (she must borrow some one's guide book) above the suave classic clock dial of zodiacal season and classically reposed woman figure underneath it, was just London. Something barbaric, giving point and reality to the somewhat overdone suavity of classic form beneath it.

Mordant had given point last summer (as had Ransome during the war-shortened period of her marriage) to her somewhat faded acceptance of realities. "You ought to have two children," shoving her own somewhat faded incompetence and old maidishness at her, "you ought to have," was Mordant's stark appraisal and his

48

somewhat Anglo-Indian brutality "children," seeing in her apparently something not quite outgrown its "usefulness," breaking into some layer of her subconscious by his stupidity. Saying "I want you to have my children," making her of some use, what use is hanging on to ideals, writing, the heady idealism that she lived by? Heady idealism grows in time sour, virgins without oil in lusterless intellectual vessels. "You ought to have two children" meant two things, actual realism of all life in its full emotional completion or actual destruction. Mordant glowering at her, bull face and ripe acceptance and infallible appraisal, someone somewhat of her own age and half-defeated fibre, having been "through" things, was a frank temptation. "He wants me to have children," she had said to Gareth. And Gareth "you're mad. Apparently you've gone mad. It's *that* … Katherine."

Gareth blamed everything on Katherine. Katherine was subterranean blue-fire, the sort of thing you think when you say Græco-Alexandrian. She was the late over-ornate winged Sphinx, a monster, all mind, having nothing to do with mind, achieving self-expression by wedding mire with mind, mind with matter, the logical conclusion of *know thyself,* haunches in the mire albeit marble haunches. Katherine was an Hellenistic monster but she *was* Hellenistic. Say Katherine even now and you saw blue mountains and you knew the somewhat problematical satisfaction of solving the Sphinx riddle would condemn you to an eternity of abandonment, emotional starvation; if you followed Katherine's tactic you sprouted premature psychic feelers, Katherine brought tiny tenuous roots out, Adonis garden to be as swiftly withered. One was all Adon-garden under Katherine's regime, all sudden premature spiritual flowering, to be as prematurely blighted. Katherine ripped souls from bodies, spiritual gynocologist. She had so endeavoured to "get at" Daniel, she had tampered with the very early pre-Gareth Raymonde. Gareth had something of Katherine's quality without her predilection for destruction. Gareth had summed up Katherine "she has the face of a dying Athenian in the pit at Syracuse ... and the instinct of a Harpy." She would gouge the soul out of any body. She had sent Raymonde, Mordant.

For reasons, Gareth insisted, for something malign and malicious. Put him up to marry, marry, knowing herself, *know thyself* means know everyone else; that is the smile on the cryptic face at Delphi. Know what will "get" Raymonde knowing what had "got" poor Katherine. For Katherine (at her own confessions) wanted to marry Mordant.

Mordant wouldn't have anything so drastic to contend with. He wanted (Gareth said) camouflage, a sort of whitewashing of the already whited sepulchre, Raymonde.

4

GOING ROUND and round, enchanted magic wheel ... dial of intrigue, something so ignoble yet something that forced open inhibition-sealed doors, doors with red seals, war seals, open the door and let down inhibition. Why hang on and on, electric fervour of intellectual integrity, where is this taking me? Say "where is this taking me" after years of valorous achievement and someone, something finds you. (With Faustus it was Mephistopheles. With Raymonde it was Katherine.) Temptation of water-blue eyes and the stricken features ... "Katherine is beautiful with the beauty of Cassandra." Someone, something crying on a stricken portico, *Know thyself* – knowing all the time that know thyself meant know everyone else ... the catch of the whole matter, says the cryptic smile at Delphi, know thyself rips self from self and leaves one self a monster. Stricken with beauty, foreknowledge that stripped husk on husk means somehow counter-magic. The gift and the withdrawal. "Know" and the world stands off, staring, fore-warned, rejecting. Men shun Cassandra. So Mordant, Katherine. Cassandra's "I'll get even" sends apprehensive shivers of pre-knowledge into the chosen vessel ... you ... you ... you ... *get even for me.*

Mordant would love Raymonde ... Raymonde would or wouldn't fall in love with Mordant ... in any case, says Katherine, "heads I win, tails you lose." But Katherine's excellent formula of "tails I win, heads you lose" was somewhat crippled. Gareth broke across with her defaming features. Garry sitting firm and secure on Florian's little tin-chair was the same Garry that had blazed at Raymonde Ransome back in London. "You ... you ... you ..." You ... you ... you chosen vessel of iniquity would be useful still for potters. Katherine wanted to break Raymonde up (Raymonde wanted to be broken) but pestle and mortar are useless against silver ... slime over the surface of intellectual integrity, let Mordant think you raw material for brick ovens. Mordant had thought her somewhat washed out clay that wanted coating with luminous vermilion. Under clay surface, something was spoiling something ... malleability was being spoiled by something.

Turn vessel, Ray Bart (Freddie called her Ray Bart) in ingenious long fingers, forefinger like bird beak, Harpy out of Asiatic cities. What's wrong with this thing? Katherine knew all along ... but it was worth trying.

Mordant saw washed-out clay colour that wanted revarnishing ... Gareth saw pure silver.

Gareth stale-mated it with her heavy feudalistic worldliness.

Raymonde hadn't taken into consideration any of her so tenuous "position." Position it appeared was something to hang on
to ... she hadn't realized she had it. "Mordant has no *position*, no
means of getting in, of getting on. He thinks you'll marry him,
coddle his pretentious little pseudo-literary ambitions." Wasn't
that temptation? It's easier to lull the threadbare second-rate into
smug contentment, lull oneself into self-effacement with it, than
to compass fresh creation. Dope artistic consciousness out of all
existence, bring carpet-slippers, mix a little night cap. Irony stalk-
ing blatant had enticed Raymonde, irony saying man, woman,
you are woman, he is apparently man. Man-woman, a temptation.
The intellect grows sterile being bi-sexual ...or a-sexual. (The very
use of the words would have frightened Mordant.) Mordant all
suppression and vibrant vitality was the mate for her then cyni-
cism. "You'd write better if you *lived* more," was his slogan then for
Raymonde. "Wh-aa-at?" "If you lived, you might really write ...
something. Not this unwholesome introspection ..." "You're quite
right." Temptation had stalked rampant, Mephistopheles with dark
eyes (as it happened) in somewhat burnt-brick visage. His colour
that ought to have been repellent radiated warmth (in London)
like bricks from Nineveh. Mordant was despotic by prepossession.
Raymonde wanted to be shut up in a harem.

Daniel had said "O Alex Mordant" and dismissed him. Daniel
had said nothing. Daniel was the crystal ball into which then Raymonde refused to be enclosed. "I won't be caught in sterile purity."
Daniel was exquisite and unworldly, Daniel was so *au fait* with the
whole gamut of affection that he simply didn't think or talk about
it. Daniel, slim rod, was the neophyte's wand. If I accept Daniel
(she had then said) I will be accepting still more intellectual initiation. I will be conversant with still more rightness out of evil. Peril

was wrapped about her. She wanted to be warm (red bricks, sun-baked in Nineveh) not climb icebergs any longer. "You're young," she had said to Daniel. "You and your sort ought to do things, create. I'm tired of writing." She had watched a face outlined with frozen features. He was some unexplored planet ridged with planet mountains. "You're far and alert and intellectualized. I'm through burning in a vacuum."

Vacuum, steadily projected, chasm between her self and Daniel. Stepping down, so to speak, into some valley layer of obliteration (Mordant, burnt Nineveh), she had by the same token, to climb and climb into the sterile mountains. Two-fold, smiling, cryptic, "I give, I withdraw," said her ever-present deity. "Know thyself" with certainty, said the omnipotent deity, you have worshipped me … if you go down, you go up. Following "know thyself" to its logical conclusion, she had found herself gasping like a fish on dry land, a mountaineer whose tried heart stops beating. She had climbed the heights intellectually, spiritually with Daniel. Two-fold initiation said the keeper of the gateway, you want to get through a door, doors are Janus-faced, two sides to initiation. Said Katherine, here is Mordant. Katherine was Cassandra, tool of Delphi.

Gareth was wrong negating Katherine's streak of authenticity. Katherine had sent Mordant to her, Katherine had sent Daniel. "I want something" had drawn its answering quarry. "I want something" is a net set in a barren wilderness, a line flung into unplumbed waters. Say "I want something" in that tone of voice (*ask and you shall receive*) and you get it. I want something; *knock and it shall be opened,* answers the Janus-faced Hebraic prophet like the deity at Delphi. Ask and you shall receive, smiles its cryptic two-sided smile at Christianity.

Ask and you shall receive ... Daniel. But it wasn't the answer anyone expected. I said I want and I want and I want. I said I am tired of intellectually scrambling up a mountain. Ask to be let down into the numbing fever smitten valley. Ask to "be let down." Deity won't let you let yourself down. Smiling, Katherine was a coin tossed. Katherine really, doing everything, had nothing to do with it. Heads I win, tails you lose. Coin flung up, fell with a pretty clatter. Spinning on its (so to speak) tail the coin had weezed and settled to its final prophecy. Mantic coin flung up, Katherine and Mordant were one side, Gareth and ... Daniel the other. Toss coin up, says the deity of Delphi, the smiling forerunner of the cryptic Jewish prophet, tails I win, heads you lose ... no matter. Coin tossed carelessly, fell just as carelessly. Gareth and Daniel faced Raymonde in Saint Mark's Square.

Gareth and Daniel were flung beside Raymonde in Saint Mark's Square. The sun fell, gold streak across London grey cloth. The sun still fell on Daniel's nordic shoulders. Head bent forward, he was seated Hermes, isles and distances were to be measured by the length of Daniel, measure antiquity by the angel-rod of Daniel. Daniel was neophyte narthex ... so far, so far ... no further. Mordant glowering affable acceptance at her had minimized endeavour. Intellect was silver-bars melted in Nineveh, claustraphobia banished ... Alex Mordant could have made me happy. Garry, symbol of intellectual vistas, was silver bars and claustraphobia ... Daniel the Elusinian wand-bearer ... so far, no further. Who knows anything of Daniel? Daniel in London had said nothing ... facing her in London ... eyes in a white set face had only said ... "try to get away if you can, from your own self." His eyes had said "go it. Good luck. I don't believe you'll do it." If Daniel had said frankly, "take care. Be careful, I must warn you against Mordant," he would have frankly fired her. His eyes were so set in their foreknowlege, the edge of his irony whetted by his indifference. "Yes. I agree with you, intense people *must* have something." Because he agreed with her, the whole thing seemed so trifling. Bronze figures on a clock tower, Gauls, barbarians, soldiers, Englishmen, Mordant and Freddie Ransome. Stupidity of Mordant who hadn't even Freddie's excuse for that thing. Soldiery was ugly, had defeated its own purpose. Mordant was really ugly.

5

SOLDIERING WAS UGLY, had defeated its own purpose. Daniel was out of it. Is it possible, said Raymonde, facing a London Daniel, that anything was out of that thing? Wait, said cryptic deity, we will need this Daniel. Daniel (soul-sperm) was flung out after the perished Freddie Ransomes and surviving Mordants. There was, it was evident, another scale of values.

I have given up sifting spiritual values, I am tired of sifting, spiritual gold-digger striking a barren sub-soil. Barren sub-soil, the just after war generation had proved so much rock and silt and little gleams of possible ore that vanished beneath one's fingers. My own people mattered but where are my own people? Gareth singularly all along remained a spiritual successor ... but Garry had married Rockway. Garry was late war and early post-war, so was Rockway. Their hard clear eyes had stared and stared at Raymonde. "Why don't you cut loose?" Post war and late war eyes (unlike the very early shattered generation) had said "hell, what's the use?" Robin Rockway with his cap tilted with remembered flying unit grace had flung his "hell" and his "hell" until even Garry, stoic and sympathetic, had recoiled. Garry was pure gun-metal. She was vibrantly metallic.

Metal endured, Garry endured where Robin Rockway failed them. Rockway with his brilliant diplomatic genius, his odd personal discernment, his cosmopolitan outlook was a shattered winged high flying plane. He felt wrecked spiritually ... perhaps he would pull himself still out of it – is spirit ever shattered? He was symbol of that crowd anyway, in or out, they had their own code. Some fell valiantly winged ... some held on. Don't try to understand them. "Hell" and "hell" and "cut loose from everything." Garry was post-war. Link on link ... Garry held true, fibre and valour but with strident inhibitions enough to drive anyone let alone poor nerve-shattered Rockway, to destruction. Garry had to be like that ... to be like that. Garry, gun-metal, held on from war to post-war. Raymonde was surviving war. Garry surviving post-war, Daniel, it was evident, was next link. Caught only at the last as a schoolboy in a training corps, Daniel was the one untainted. They were all tainted ... but this Daniel.

Daniel would "carry on," it was evident, if they would hold together. Garry links me up to the post-war people, I link Garry up to the war people. We have held on sometimes hating each other ... as now. Now Garry and I are hating each other ... we must hold on for Daniel.

THE YEAR moved backward ... the year moved suddenly forward. The year went zip, zip, zip, swiftly past the quarter, the half, the three quarter ... they were back in Venice. This is here, now, said Raymonde, watching the boy pose the girl (girl and boy escapade, were they off the Swedish Nord Stirn?) on the slab about the middle centre lamp post. The girl (from the Nord Stirn?) dropped corn kernels, the pigeons obligingly pecked. The boy said "good, Gladys," so evidently they were not off the Nord Stirn, but momentarily dissociated perhaps from the Cook crowd, hot from the Campanile, just now debouching (Camberwell, Camden Town) from the Campanile corner. The Cook crowd (the boy and girl had joined them) cut through an irregular trail of black shirts that just now emerged, highly dramatic, from the Piazetti dei Leoni. Small, smaller, smallest boys trailed after the cue's barrage, ridiculous, like dressed monkeys. Black pirates, the Fascisti made Saint Mark's Square alien to Italy; United Italy, this thing belongs to people off boats. It seemed the right of all the people off boats to shoo away Fascisti. This place belongs to people drinking vermouth or tea or lemonade at Florian's or Aurora's little tables, or the ones across the way whatever that place is called, where they play nothing but Trovatore. People, pigeons, who were these Fascist black-shirts? Crows had descended, a black flock, settled among garden colours. "Shoo off the Fascisti." "Wh-aa-at's the matter, Raymonde? Don't talk like that." "I wasn't saying anything." "You said shoo off the Fascisti."

The year moved forward, it was (it was evident) this year, it was now, here. The sun fell warm on Daniel's London shoulders. The sun left a bar now where it had fallen full weight, the touch of mantic fingers. "The sun's gone from your shoulder, Daniel." Daniel looked up, he seemed never to have moved, all that time ... while time sped its reckless dial pace from last year to this year, now here. "Time it's apparent, is irrelevant." "Wh-aa-at?" "What, *what* exactly Garry?" "You said something was irrelevant. I wish you wouldn't shout so."

Garry was telling her that she must be more careful. Garry of the "O hell" generation was saying Raymonde must be circumspect, be careful. Careful. What was careful? The clock was dinging again ... bronze Gauls on the clock tower were side stepping out to ring little bronze bells, great notes over the sun-steeped piazza, this year, now here. Bells rang, it is here, it is this year. The sun would soon be setting. It couldn't conceivably go on pouring bars and rays of heavy molten gold in layers out of an old-fashioned steel engraving. There was nothing but gold bars ... as last night bars of silver. "Everything's exaggerated. Do you remember last night?" Garry wasn't going to enthuse with anybody. Daniel was feeding pigeons. I must go on alone, thought Raymonde. Won't any one help me bear it? I love Venice too much.

The sun for all its dynamic heat, weighing them all down, would soon be setting. It would go suddenly, drop behind the campanile, drop suddenly behind the other (Georgio Maggiore) bell tower, drop swiftly behind the Giudecca. The sun would soon go suddenly but mites still swarmed within it ... people ... people ... in the porches of the piazzetta, in and out of the cathedral doorways. People swarmed and people drifted ... Brixton and Camberwell (with the boy and Gladys) had disappeared quite suddenly while fresh Camberwells and Brixtons drifted (how can there be so many?) with Minneapolis, South Dakota, Winnipeg and Valparaiso, from the symmetrical *calle* leading out of Saint Mark's Square; odd (to mix metaphor) sea creatures drifted ... insects in pollen gold dust became sea-creatures, drift, drifting from somewhat shaken sea centres, wondering vaguely (to mix metaphor) what high-tide of fortune had deposited them at the foot of the campanile, before cathedral gateways. The look of surprise on white London faces was the same look of surprise on American faces gone dark with the spring sea-voyage, of Surbiton and Chatauqua faces, of Chicago and Minneapolis faces, things over the other side, remember what we've come from, how have we got here? "How have we got here" never left one alone to say "this is a clever face" or "this is a haughty face" or "this face shows years of turmoil" or "this face is merely vapid." Raymonde was debauched with the whole spectacle, "*how* have we got here" … faces, people all had a look of familiarity, of common denominator awareness, of surprise that just this thing should have overtaken them to their little odd back-water of Minneapolis, Berlin or Copenhagen. Debauched faces meeting debauched faces in the square were all somehow standardized, wearing one mask of sunlight, were odd (to mix metaphor) fish out of their element, flung by some sea-fortune into one pool, turning on themselves after some strife and some little wonder of readjustment, to stand upright, so to speak, on their tails and see whatever else it was that this same sea-tide, so favoring them, had flung in here beside them. The lowest or the highest common denominator was in all their faces. This is the thing – this is the thing – the blocked-in outline familiar from cheap tourist folders, or slap-dash posters, in railway terminals, Winnipeg, Valparaiso, come true, come *right* under one's very sea-wind sniffing nostrils. Classic Venice, romantic Venice (Raymonde was debauched with the whole spectacle) poster Venice, post-card Venice, Othello Venice, clap-trap stage Rialto Venice became real ("what news o' the Rialto?"); Elizabeth Barrett Browning and Wagner and Duse and George Sand Venice (she was frankly reeling with it) came true, became so many sets of feelings to be coped with, the feelings that made just those people come here, what they felt when here, still went on here; differentiate one from one, how Heine must have felt sitting just here, how Wagner. What must have been George Sand's reaction to just that sort of scr-aa-atch in the air the pigeons wing-points made in passing; bird wings scratched the very molten substance of that sunlight. Sunlight fell on all, obliterating ... while miraculous ice forms remained unmelted in it, column and pillars and sets of separate pillars, the marbles of Saint Mark's Cathedral doorway. Mirage frozen ... Saint Mark's Cathedral doorway.

Blocks of marble enclosed green fronds; stalactites, marble slab and inset triangle and rhomboid; column, twisted little group of columns and eclectic device on shield or carved coat of arms – Colleoni? Stampalia? names, people, jumble of moss and sea-weed; amber pattern on a stone water step. Seaweed and sea-drifting creatures ... dolphins curvetted and smiled at – dolphins – people, so many odd fish from so many foreign waters, all collected in little shoals, in little fish-clusters, a black shoal from the North Sea or a dark blue shoal from mid-Atlantic or a white shoal of people off Mediterranean boats in summer dresses. Umbrellas unfurled, sea-anemone shapes, blobs of colours static or heaving as if washed over by iridescent sub-marine tropic waters. Sea-green, sea-blue, rock and sea and stone and Surbiton posing for its portrait. "She's actually got a dove to sit on her wrong-end of Oxford Street felt hat."

6

NOW THERE was no seaweed to it, it was all a garden ... now there was no garden ... it was one huge dynamo ... the excitement of watching what might happen to other people, spiritual clap-trap, the sort of spiritual joke of the thing that had its parallel in remembered antics of a Coney Island side show ... electric-charged side-walk and the people who had been "had" watching those who were in the state of being "had." Electric radiators under the piazza paving stones and the crudely initiated waiting in a state of permanent grin the advent of new victims. Something happens to everybody. They were all Marco Polos about to be dynamized into activity.

Marco Polo came back from the Orient to sit here; electric fervour, all the impulse that had driven Marco Polo to the Orient still throbbed here; vibration, steady and undeviating, still pulsed and drove people toward intellectual harbours of appreciation. Vibration, electric thing beneath them, throb-throb, steamer in mid-ocean, vibration, impulse toward understanding, spiritual comprehension, actual illumination. Pulse-pulse; they all seemed (atoms clustered about Florian's little tables) sitting on a huge dynamo, anything might happen; they were being re-created, heated above, beneath, "incubated" from some vibrant centre. They'd hatch soon, awkward chicks, flamingo-coloured, breaking the shell, Winnipeg or Valparaiso. "Athens is played out" Raymonde found herself surreptitiously pronouncing, barely breathing (it was as well Garry hadn't heard her) Athens vibrates too high (she got it suddenly). Greek vibration is ultraviolet ... the sort of thing you sense with some super-vibratory nerve centre, piercing, shattering; the inhumanity of spirit. Greek light pierced, harrowed one to more intense flight; this sustained, held one enclosed, smothered down in beauty, suffocated, painlessly snuffed out, one's only exaltation being this loss of one's identity; loss of identity was the gift of Venice.

Greek genius is white lightning across daylight skies, lightning across already intolerable light, it was obvious how this sustained summerday heat had brought golden Veronese to flower, Palma Vecchio, tiger-lily Tintoretto. Lilies ... she was back now with a garden ... sea anemone sunshades were so many lilies and the

61

place was full of sounds that fill lilies, that radiate about lilies in late-summer gardens (Venetian painters are late-summer paint-ers) leaf-sound, bee-sound, earth-sound of crickets, katydids, but-terflies with furled butterfly coloured wings. Each bit of rumpled ribbon or lining of a bag flung open on a table or bright catch on another hand bag was manifestation of butterfly colour, insectiver-ous wing quiver of a hawk-moth, metallic green knob of a beetle. "I don't know why I didn't care for Venice" ... she did know why she hadn't before this cared especially for Venice. If you just aren't keyed, attuned to this suave dynamo of vibration, the place is com-mon-place. People, things exist in relation to the understanding; they don't exist obviously, unless you exist, dynamo of comprehen-sion, catching dynamo spark from the object you're attuned to. "I don't know. I do know. I loved Florence." (Florentine painters – it came suddenly – are April painters.) "Perhaps one couldn't love the two together." Divided Italy has meant partisanship, perhaps that partisanship existed still in spirit. You give your soul to one thing, you can't give it to another.

7

YET IS THAT true? She had given her soul to Gareth, she had given her soul to Daniel. Inappositely it was Daniel who was Flor-ence, Tuscan fidelity, intellectual subtlety, clairvoyant physical intuition. Daniel said he would sooner *not* be found dead in Flor-ence. Gareth went out of her way to jibe at Bellini, to attempt to scratch with intellectual contempt that quaint Harlequin of paint-ers (Ruskin's phrase) Carpaccio. Garry's very sincere back-talk at the expense of Tintoretto made him seem a living person; they were all so real to Gareth in her hatred. Hatred or fear (another name for hatred) of the thing that she was. Gareth was that special Bellini in the Accademia, the sort of effect of small cherubs, raspberry shaped small Erotes, raspberry coloured sort of bee-wings to astral coloured angels. Gareth was Bellini. If Raymonde burnt a candle surreptitiously to Bellini (say in Saint Zacharia's) she found expression for her belated love of Gareth. Gareth was this thing. Raymonde had found formula for Gareth. Gareth was, it was obvious, the Bellini side of Venice as Daniel was obviously the Verrochio Mina da Fiesole side of Florence. Daniel had made a detour to escape Florence, he wouldn't on any account ever "be found dead there." Gareth had corne to Venice only on the distinct understanding that it was a *faux de mieux,* a port of landing, a stepping stone out to more sympathetic milieu … sympathetic? That was the catch of the whole complicated matter. Vibration of Saint Mark's Square wasn't reaching Gareth.

AGES KEEP COMING up into ages where they don't belong, Raymonde was stricken with it, ghost ages like the dove in the light globe, Tintoretto swings, dove-sun into his barn annunciation in the Scuolo di San Rocco. Belated vision stalked blatant in Saint Mark's Square, belated words preserved in amber, words in amber melted in that sunlight … Greek words gone heady, life within life, Greek words "consider the birds" were sap, gold from a heavy tree, forest tree of Judaic, of Greek mythology. Philosophy was a great tree and words were flowing out, fragrant words, tree sap, maple trees merging to pine-trees near the water … there were pine trees near the water … but it was only flag poles. Her mind re-adjusted, contemplated naked flag poles, pine trees stripped of leafage. Malappropriate foliage, banners dripped from the three upstanding flag poles, stark green and red, poster-green and poster-red of the two Italian flags, and in the centre a third blatantly stressing the crude vulgarity of the others, the worn old-gold and leaf-gold of the ancient winged-lion-paw-on-a-book banner of the republic. Flags folding, unfolding before cathedral portals, reminded Raymonde of deciduous leafage and ... Gareth is unhappy.

IT WAS HORRIBLE of Gareth to mar this thing with bickering, to cut across the clear relationship they had established. Strangers met, had met last year in London, she and Gareth, had become strangers after five years' separation. Strangers more than brothers, like Hindoo lovers meeting in after lives, after vivid incarnations, to exploit and compare past experience. You ... you ... you ... you look the same, are the same Garry. You ... you ... you ... you look different, aren't the same, Ray Bart and their quarrel had begun as far back as last summer ... London ... so much further away than the not so distant, problematic Athens. They had quarrelled then about Mordant, about Katherine. Katherine was responsible for the whole fiasco, Garry had insisted – but why drag it all, with all its connotations, back into this blessed sunlight ... let Gareth stay a stranger, not come too close. The stranger, Gareth, the intellectual almost-twin was a creature of swift parallel thought lines running straight with her lines as if she had been (it seemed now that she had Gareth) all the intermediate years she had existed without Gareth, a useless direct thing, with all its integrity utterly useless like one single arrow-like line of prolonged double rails, half a railroad running straight into some sudden wilderness. Now that she had Gareth, the intellectual track of her endeavour seemed to have been justified. There was, had been all the time, although she had not known it, another just such rail, running along with her rail.

64

Intellectually she and Gareth made one track across a desert, but morally, ethically, spiritually – Garry was sulking like a little girl. The thing hurt horribly.

Raymonde must propitiate Gareth, get her into it for somehow suddenly it seemed to her (herself so melted into heady molten sunlight) it was the person most unhappy that most mattered. Daniel couldn't matter, being molten with her, one substance with her; Garry was really bee-wings if she would let herself be bee-wings, she was an astral-coloured raspberry shaped ridiculous small angel with the war gear of Athene. Garry was ridiculous, was disproportionate. Garry was unhappy, "yes, Garry I know," propitiate, explain, be false in the gift (propitiation) but not false in the spirit that prompted propitiation. "I always *did* say I didn't care for Venice." Throw out with false frankness, this "between ourselves one must keep up a sort of bluff of appreciation," art and art and what is expected of one; throw the thing out with hearty falseness and even as Raymonde spoke firm-founded in her pre-conception that whatever self in her self she played false to, she wouldn't play false to her loyalty to Gareth, there was a whirring as of æons. Aeons brushed through her ... pigeons from niche, from coppice, from edges of Corinthian capitals and from Palladio statue bases. Pigeons emerged like bees from honey-comb sud-denly for no reason that one could see (not the excuse of that orgy of established noon-grain) motivated by some common impulse. Pigeons emerged like bees from honey-comb, buzzing, burrowing into sunlight like flies, like bees into some molten amber. Things moved in this amber, saint-like, god-like – Saint Anne with Sis-tine Sibyl eyes came toward them ... "that old thing's come back," clock-circle of Saint Mark's Square, "the tiresome old woman" proffering carefully doctored blossoms. Buzzing, burrowing,

burrowing into sunlight, into saint-light. Yet seen the other way round, picture post-card, "vulgar tourists" cheap poster gaudiness of colour, cheap green, poster-red of the Italian flag, crude, played out, horribly shown up beside the middle ancient paw-on-a-book Venetian republic banner.

Things showed up terribly, things were shown up by things, you could rip the whole show to rags with a bit of clear analysis (Garry was quite right) seen the other way round the whole thing was preposterous. Everything in the whole, equally everything in detail, everything was preposterous, the wired carnations for instance in the old hag's basket, looked as if they had been dipped in red ink, picture post-card carnations, streaked with as blatant crudity as the green, red, white of the king's flag. Paper carnations, paper carnival roses were hardly, were they, flowers? Raymonde said, "they aren't, are they, flowers?" and realized she was off the track, going off the rails, off the tangent and she was talking to Gareth, realizing that Gareth and she had spread wide wings or she had spread wide wings and Garry (this was the horror of it) hadn't. Garry was sulking visibly in sun-light.

8

"SO DO YOU remember ... do you remember ..." Raymonde hazarded, get Garry into it. Let Daniel realize there were years of intimate concord, conflict or communion (it didn't matter) between her and Gareth. "Garry do you remember ..." anything, it didn't matter, the Lynmouth Bretts and their hateful foster-son, that man who ate bananas with hot milk all the way over on the Atlantide, the two sailors that they took the collection for at the hotel (she had forgotten the name) at San Antonio. Make little side allusions and carefully and politely afterwards, with well-bred implication, explain them all to Daniel. Let Daniel see that she and Gareth were a sort of composite person she and Gareth, Raymondegareth or Garethraymonde, a person that had existed (Raymondegareth) before ever there was a Daniel. Let Daniel who was so terribly, terribly in it seem out of it precisely. "O Garry," Raymonde achieved a stage peal of actual almost-hysteria, "that woman there with the dyed ostrich boa looks so terribly like Frieda Hochensteiner." Explain this particular allusion (Gareth was smiling faintly) exaggerate the importance of it, elaborate, appliqué allusion on it, get Daniel out of it.

Make Frieda Hochensteiner seem important though she never was important. Explain it, make a diagram, re-embroider on fresh frame-work, this year and this summer year and this golden sea year and this year before that when Renée Stark got married. People, things, network of places, people, she and Gareth were linked, nothing could interfere, not even Daniel who was so terribly part of it, webbed into it treasonably, silver web of exquisite silk texture that shelters problematic twin grubs. She and Gareth were somehow dark things beside the thing called … Daniel. But they were twin things, had been twin things, Garethraymonde, Raymondegareth before there was a Daniel.

But it wasn't Daniel, whirr of wings entreated, you and Garry and Daniel were happy before you came to Venice. Venice. Before you came to Venice. Treason was prowling somewhere … Daniel mustn't break across them, but it wasn't Daniel, it was a more illusive, composite thing, a sort of superimposition, like vision superimposed on vision in some exquisite improbable screen version of something altogether out of the world and altogether not to be grappled with in mere crude language ... something composite that was whirr of wings, that was furled and unfurled sun shades, that was the fact that nothing of the Orient (Marco Polo must have thought) held such charm, such dope simply as this thing: Saint Mark's Square set palpable, improbable in sunlight.

... bees hung, they must be doing, in the air above them. Whirr of wings that must tear the heat, let it drip like the middle banner in gold streamers. The middle banner of the three banners before Saint Mark's, dripped and flung its gilt edge against the middle flag-pole and the ends hung there, heavy as if the pole itself were some tall, slender exotic tree dripping exotic red leaves and gold leaves, dripping, dripping ... they were being swallowed in it (she and Daniel) and Gareth wasn't. This was the terrible thing. Gareth was out of it.

Firmly incarnated, incarcerated almost you might have thought in her steel grey travelling costume (no bee-wings visible) hard perfect tailored lines of firm small square shoulders ... Garry was Athene sitting in a London costume sulking visibly in sunlight. "Pallas Athene when she was angry produced incarnate anger." "Wha-aat?" "I said when Pallas Athene was angry she *was* angry." A Gorgon had stared at her ... Garry was frightening but Garry shouldn't spoil this. Gareth rolled things up like you might that middle silken banner. The banner momentarily hiding and reveal-ing that cathedral doorway, made a sort of drop-curtain, stressing dramatic interval, so that for a moment one was right with one set of values, Gareth, the mind, her singular acumen and the fact that in London she saved me, got me out of that vicious Mordant-Katherine cycle, and the next moment, (flap) one's mental outfit changed, one's values shifted. Time was indicated by this drop-curtain that rose, that fell, making moments into æons again, this odd facility of dramatizing everything that was the gift of Venice; moods were dramatized, time sequence stressed, that flap and that flap of gold and crimson on a flag pole. "Gareth is worth all this mumbo-jumbo" one capitulated, facing those glazed Gorgon eyes in heady sunlight, remembering the intellectual stimulus they brought one, "all this incense and little carved naked cupids holding up sacred founts" and then (flap) Garry wasn't. "Classic blurred by late ornate colour and the late ornate quality that you get *true* in Florence" one conceded, "here is all gone to seed, great lilies, over-ripe, red and orange and everything about to fall like crimson leaves, ripe leaves, just not-rotten." The minute that came clear above or across the buzzing of wings (the usual pigeons) the formula was no good. The minute one said "Pallidio is no good, Garry is everything" the lion-paw-on-a-book banner of the Republic flapped apart, made a new scene. Every time the wind lifted it, blowing fresh down the funnel-like Piazetta from the lagoon and the Grand Canal, something *changed*. Every time the wind blew the symmetrically a-symmetrical fringes of the banner across the far side of the cathedral and the stone lions and the fountain and those other pigeons gathered on the carved raised well-head like flies on honey-comb or small quite ordinary day-moths on a flat flower, something dynamically altered. There was never getting anything straight. Every word made a change, pebbles dropped into deep waters, pebbles dropped into shallow water, everybody's words, not only Garry's, the words of the officer at the next table ... going on and on, Italian is voweled in spite of people constricting that special water-over-stones quality to Greek ..." I mean, it was spoiled for me that last time. Just rushing in to get the boat – everything spoiled and the time before ..." Raymonde, it was evident, was whole-heartedly enchanted, swept into this vivid

cycle, every word she spoke, it seemed, was about to change infini-
ties. Pebbles dropped into placid water, rings of thought, rings of
water-like concentric circles that thought takes over the blur and
buzz of colour in Saint Mark's Square, were changed by the mere
vibration sound made in speaking. Not my voice only ... their
voices. Wound round in a web of magic, just keep Gareth quiet,
don't try actually to cope with Garry, "last time everything was
spoiled" (say anything) "with all that pother about the Kerr-Webbs
missing their boat to Constan."

9

THERE WAS NO use saying this is true or this is true. Nothing
was true anywhere. Or everywhere everything was true. It was true
eclectically that Garry had stalked into her apartment one day in
London when things had reached their critical last climax and had
said "clear out Raymonde." Garry like a sword flashing through
late London mist (mist seeped into her little top floor London
eerie; she always stayed too late) had driven Raymonde out, out.
Eve naked with her one intellectual, so to speak, garment of the
tried spirit into the ... wilderness, "I don't want to go. I am fed up
with writing." Garry had flayed her forth, out of the "sticky drug
of the Katherine-Mordant cycle" (Garry would never give Katherine credit for authenticity) into the ... wilderness. "I'll be so ... so
cold in d'y Vaud." Garry had driven her out, and up problematic
intellectual icebergs and as if to make up for all that, after three
months' stoic and horrible seclusion, had wired her, somehow
telepathically knowing that she was sick to death of herself and of
non-achievement, to join up with her in Venice in order to take

a boat (they would discuss that later) somewhere. Garry's letters following straightaway had made clear that Raymonde wasn't to bother about all the worry of the (as Garry tactfully put it) "extras" … so here I am more or less Garry's guest, Raymonde's mind would keep on insisting, this year's income shockingly overdrawn, little enough in all consciousness but not enough for that sort of shoddy extravagance Mordant let me into. Dresses, the wrong kind, all shoddy and extreme and all the paraphernalia of keeping life from sinking. I was shoddy and extravagant in London, income overdrawn, ambition gone, I said "let everything go, Katherine is really right in these particulars" and Garry burst upon me. Garry was uncanny, had been acute and devastatingly accurate in her analysis. "It isn't this swine Mordant that you think you love, it's Ransome." "Wh-aa-at? I thought you hated Freddie." "I did. I do. He stood for the worst of England … that idiotic rotten public school attitude … and System. But at least he had the decency to die for his convictions." "It wasn't Alex Mordant's fault that he wasn't killed at Vimy." "Vimy? Vi-iii-my? Blimy. He never yet saw Vimy." "It's none anyhow of your, Garry, business." "Your business is my business …" "Your people shall be my people and your …" Raymonde had begun mockingly but she couldn't finish. Facing Garry in that surcharged little London apartment where too much always happened, she couldn't be just funny, remembering too much. What had Garry done for her in the past? What had Garry done, what wouldn't Garry have done to have saved her from all the hideous war fiasco? Garry would have put her two small hands heroically into a red flame … but it wouldn't have helped … anybody. Raymonde would have let herself be sliced piece by piece for Garry … but Garry married Rockway. "You and I had to know … we had to *know* Garry." Knowledge holds out problematical inducements. Delphic Helios backed by all too one-sided Athene. Athene before the portals, Pronaos, that is what she was, what Garry was. Katherine after all was something on her own, a whim of some divinity. Katherine was Cassandra, follow her prophecy … believing. "I believe in Katherine." "Katherine wants to blight you." "How can anybody blight anybody? We are each his own three fates, each spinning his own pattern." "You spin rottenly." "How – rottenly?" "Vimy. Blimy. We had that Mordant pattern only something decent … once. It's war-reversion. You are reverted and introverted. You think by marrying Mordant or by being his greasy mistress, that you'll get back – " "Get back?" "The lost … that is lost."

Whither thou goest I will go, and where thou lodgest, I will lodge … but it meant going alone to d'y Vaud, an icy winter …, nobody there, Daniel couldn't help her … pouring over pages and pages … I've lost time, I've slid back … and Garry's telegram at the last after three winter months and barren non-achievement, "I'm going on a Mediterranean cruise, somewhere. I want company. You come." All very vague, meaning nothing, meaning everything, meaning in particular shoving listlessly a few rags into a handbag and sliding through the Simplon. To find Daniel standing beside Garry outside the Ferrovia and Venice as Venice never had been … beautiful.

The sun being hot on her face nothing mattered … she had left the face that she might have wanted to hide, in London, pre-Raphaelite effect for a demodé Mordant. Candles on candlesticks and the sort of thing she knew Katherine had led Mordant to expect she would aspire to. "O this new art … monstrous." Cigarette holder in proportion to the decor and her hair frayed out, all unlike her. A listless, somewhat dreary, obvious Raymonde. (What in London, anyhow could Daniel ever matter?) "O that boy Daniel Kinoull. Yes. I – like – him." She had said she liked Daniel Kinoull to a heady Mordant. Then having said she liked him she wondered why she had said that ... the other was as easy, more non-committal. Arguing in herself, she realized that she did not want to commit Daniel to this Mordant and became fulsome, "charming boy ... a sweet, sweet friend to Katherine." Slurring over the emphasis so that it might mean anything and Mordant was down on her ... gouging bull with the instinct of a blood-hound. Gouge the thing to death ... gouge Daniel to destruction. And suddenly Daniel meant something to her ... malleable, he was to be held, crystal before a furnace. Knowing furnace heat can not mar crystal but rather more refine it, she had turned this Daniel round and round, a crystal cup before this heady Mordant. Mordant was heady furnace before which (she had that satisfaction) she had shaped molten substance, finally as ... Daniel. "Daniel is so – eclectic."

Mordant wouldn't know what eclectic meant ... but it did for Mordant. She was eclectic, Katherine was eclectic ... (O they were all eclectic and hieratic and daemonic and all those things besides this commonplace full blooded Alex Mordant who yet had power to make poor Katherine love him. They were superimposed like two mystic triangles, the two triangles that make a star, the seal of Solomon. Triangle pointing up, triangle pointing down ... the seal of utter wisdom. Alex Mordant, Katherine, Raymonde ... then Raymonde again (the Ray Bart of Gareth's predilection) Gareth and Daniel. Raymonde doubled the role ... they made a star between them.

Rip triangle from triangle ... get out of London. Leave a frazzled weary simulacra of an image behind in the heart of Mordant. "An odd woman ... you know ... not altogether wholesome."

The sun being hot on her face … now here, here now in Venice nothing mattered. Here, now, things kept ringing from somewhere else, distinct bell sounds, sound on sound as if one deep bell had an echo, another slice of somewhere echoed back that echo, the very sunlight made wall against which resonous bells re-echoed. Now, here … sunlight melted frozen Alpine features, sunlight dried off the fog and stench of former Londons. Now here, Pythian sun-god shot arrows … all evil is simply dried out … Python discontent, I am being re-made.

Re-made, ready made, unmade she knew Italians loved her … in particular the group of officers, pretending not to see her, one in the middle, older with a bald head, with thin wolf lips, the mouth of some Appian werewolf, hungry, sun-steeped, how can this old, old "decadent" race be so incredibly virile? Anglo-Saxons seemed played out (though obviously Daniel wasn't that nor Gareth) with fog-steeped features; wine-coloured tunics should flow from such limbs … they were really werewolfish were Italians. Things being true weren't true. She was part of both the cycles.

She was part of the commonness of the three officers … they were utterly pretentious. She was part of the thing that made them aristocratic. (Illusion is renewed here.) She wanted to keep up her double role, base and tip of the pyramid at the same moment, up pointing and down pointing triangle of the star-seal of Solomon. "I am part of those three Italians." "Wh-a-at?" "Those three officers." "Don't be incredibly low, Raymonde." "I mean they see I see." You see, I see, they see, we see. There was no you, I or they anywhere. The only thing that made an I, that was spiked round with I-ness was Gareth. I, I, I spiked round Garry like a porcupine with prickles. Raymonde said "you're a porcupine with prickles" for Garry was saying, "I hate these smug Italians. I loathe Italy."

How could anyone loathe this thing called Venice? Gareth wasn't hating Venice, it was Gareth's phobia that was hating Venice. Gareth's phobia was armour plate about Gareth and Gareth, bee-wings, was about to be crushed by this heavy phobia of Gareth. Break Gareth from her phobia, how to break Gareth from her phobia? Under the armour plate, Gareth was being injured ... don't argue ... there's nothing to do but to soak up sunlight. I'm like a huge dry dusty sponge that's been put back into its element ... inapposite simile but I'm like that, only the sun is molten flowing in, around. I'm soaking up sunlight like a dry sponge water. "Garry, don't be insufferable."

Raymonde said "Garry, don't be insufferable" but Garry hadn't heard her. Garry had switched off, so to speak, the light ... the connection between Garry and Garry was somehow disconnected. What can I do, what can I do, cried Raymonde, but there wasn't any use trying to do anything. She was in the wrong. I am in the wrong ... a sort of guest of Gareth. Garry had wired her, come along, don't worry about "extras" for all her this year's income was madly overdrawn, that insuperable waste with Mordant. Dresses rumpled and flung aside ... that hideous bead thing he so liked. The more expensive a frock the more hideous ... insufferable pseudo mondanity ... Mordant had excruciating taste ... wasted effort. Well, you can not serve ... God and ... Gareth. I am a pure sun-worshipper ... consider the birds ... Gareth isn't. I wish Gareth weren't such an intolerable little megalomaniac.

The flower vendor, vendoress, the old Sibyl hag had come back, counter clock-wise, making her clock and counter clock circuit of Saint Mark's Square. Her basket was the same, her flowers were the same. Was her basket the same? Things fitted in things, double triangle, the up and the down, the specifically trivial and the mystically illuminating. Flowers and basket changed ... illusion was at work on paper-coloured flowers.

Things changed things ... footsteps, voices, pebbles dropped into widening circles, cycles, seasons as if that old Sibyl's circle of the square had made zodiac season circle, carefully compassed in the set space of geometric parallel, parallelogram, people were cut in slices by zodiac passing. "Illusion is renewed here" twinkled back at Raymonde in the stage flung-in eye-glass of the bald central most Roman of the three Italian officers. She was enclosed in understanding, in the understanding of all Italy. Viva Italia, that vulgar red and poster-green war cry of the Savoia. Gareth was right. "They *are* vulgar." Illusion encompassed her. Garry shouldn't know this.

Garry spoke acidly, ignoring (to Garry) too, too obvious truism about the seated soldiers, "that old hag said this time 'get roses for the young man'. " "Wh-aaat?" Raymonde heard her voice across Gareth's scornful voice, " she couldn't have. Not in – in Venice." "She said Signore." "O – signore – plural – ladies. Us. She says get carnations – " "It was roses – " " – for the ladies."

10

BUT NOTHING mattered, viva Savoia or viva Gareth or viva anything except just this exquisite aura of reality. The very earth seemed to be ringed with a saint's halo, light ringed Saint Mark's Square, patently the aura of some god-head, there wasn't room for bickering. "She said Signore." "O – signore – plural – ladies. Us. She says get carnations – " "It was roses – " " – for the ladies."

An echo of an echo of an echo of a quarrel. The words before they were spoken really had already formed an echo of an echo; hold this little quarrel to your ear, Raymonde, listen to an echo of an echo. This is the clue to something, something about Garry. Get Garry out of her phobia as you might prod a winkle from its shell, get Garry from her phobia. "She *said* Signore." Hold shell to your ear, words are only a shell of something other, echo upon echo upon echo ... Raymonde couldn't catch it. There's something wrong with Garry. If I could analyse her as she did me, cruelly, crudely, dynamically it might be all right. But Garry is so composite, so apparently simple, so very, very trying. To get Garry from her phobia would be a question of inhuman (which I haven't) patience. I suppose it was Robin Rockway, something he did ... O God.

But all that didn't matter, none of that mattered really. Husbands and wars didn't matter, death and estrangement didn't matter. The thing that really mattered, the only thing that could matter in the whole world was that a new sun-shade had opened in Saint Mark's Square, another parasol, quite a different shade (incredible) from any other. Now what colour is that sun-shade? You might call it crimson but crimson wouldn't answer. Then how about magenta? Well magenta doesn't sound right, ah ... it's ... *fuchsia*. A fuchsia-coloured sun-shade, fresh opened in Saint Mark's Square was more important than wars and differences. Death and estrangement can't really matter in Saint Mark's Square. Two prim English women, escaped so to speak, from some provincial garden, some sweet scented dried-out sort of rock-border, sort of thrift herb, almost flowerless, profited by their emancipation from prim gardens to flower riotously. The Italianated Englishman is the devil. So the Italianated English old-maid, thought Raymonde ... how wonderful for them ... in Saint Mark's Square.

They were having really the very devil of a time in Saint Mark's

Square. Just being there, having counted their handkerchiefs and their stout stockings carefully this morning, having locked up the silver link bag and the pinchbeck locket (it was our poor mother's) and having primly demanded in guide-book Italian their week's pension bill, they felt the very devils. Things weren't as bad as they had half-expected, Fascisti had cleared *that* up. The Fascisti you know, my dear, corresponds to our church boy's brigade and really that is something ... "there are 710 beggars" the one with button boots must have written to the vicar and the other, "my dear, dear Mr. Ridgway-Frith, you may think it too, too dreadful. I couldn't resist yesterday the holy water." Their letters would be read by the sewing society ... those dear Miss Strothers. Miss Strothers and Miss Veronica Strothers were basking in Saint Mark's Square royally.

We are lizards escaped from shells ... we are birds (Winnipeg, Valparaiso) hatched royally. We are all hatched but Garry. If Garry hatched she would be bee-winged, a sort of raspberry sort of as-tral-coloured angel. I can't prod out Garry. She must be incubated. I wish she would just let go like the Miss Smithers or the Miss Strothers from Newcastle-on-Tyne or Ashton-under-Lyme. The Miss Strothers or Miss Smithers were sitting sideways, like sitting wrong way round in a theatre, not noticing they were noticed (but they weren't in that sense noticed) sitting sideways like people in a box, looking at Saint Mark's. The fuchsia sun-shade cast fuchsia colour on the face of the younger and her eyes were steadfast, Nor-dic grey eyes, stupid prim mouth (stupid people matter) Nordic eyes staring and staring at Saint Mark's cathedral. Say again "Saint Mark's is too horribly like the postcards" for Raymonde was so happy, go back to that "ten-cent store box of blocks," be facetious, giggle. Shout out very loud as if to an assembled audience, hoping to placate Garry, "the whole place is preposterous" for the whole thing was so a sort of saint's aura to its own banality, that if Gareth knew even now how terribly Raymonde was involved with all of it, how horribly and completely, she was, as it were, compromised by all this beauty, Gareth would be beyond all reason, angry. Gareth sensed, obviously, with her uncanny sixth-sense, just what the place was doing, not quite what it *had* done. The place has changed me utterly, people used to go on pilgrimages, this is how it changed them. You hatch out before you know it … make some remark to Daniel, "I do know what Gareth means about the Grand Canal. It is, in that sense, terrible."

The face of Daniel lifted to meet her face. He had been breaking brioche, so extravagant. Gareth had said and she had said "but buy a little cornucopia of grain from that little man, they all do, it's better." Daniel's face lifted to meet her face. Daniel was trying to get crumbs across to the lame dove, the one that hopped and came just so far, and then back-slid on its worn tail, sliding back like a skidding bus across the square flags and waiting beside a great empty space, disappearing and re-emerging, never getting closer. "Life" Daniel had said "stepped on that bird and he never got over it." Daniel had been extravagantly throwing brioche crumbs to the lame pigeon that hopped, its shoulder hunching, terrible little journey from a chair leg to the little spike, spread claw-wise, that was the table leg, to the next chair, to the next spike of three, to the next, to skid again at the sight of a mountain foot emerging suddenly. Daniel looked up. His hands hung limp between his grey knees. "Elegant long line from the waist to the floor" as she had once described that curious frail length to him, making his eyes dilate a moment, and his eyelids wait a moment and then close like shutters, shutting out some secret, something so dear and personal, his way of seeing a joke. Daniel was looking at her. His eyes were set in his face rather like the eyes of the younger of the two prim English women (Miss Veronica?) who had almost forgotten to be prim under the fuchsia sun-shade. His eyes were blank, just rather zinc-coloured cold bits of metal, somehow self-shuttered. Behind the eyes, Daniel was waiting, the Daniel who said "life stepped on that bird. He never got over it."

"Did you get your bird its brioche?" Daniel said "one crumb out of say, fifty odd tossed bits. He did get one crumb." "A crumb to a bird," she rallied to it, "must be as big as a biscuit. Like a small *petit-pain*. He's had his." The sun seemed hanging, everlastingly hanging, invisible in mid air somewhere. Yet all the time the sun had been sliding gradually ... had now slid ... she wouldn't have noticed it if the elder of the two very devils of Italianated old-maids hadn't furled her fuchsia sun-shade. "I mean nothing matters here. Everything matters. It's like God. Consider the birds ..." now she was frightened at this. "I mean the cathedral and the lagoons and the sky all seem part of a plan, something planned, and we are part of a vast plan, no more important than the lame bird, even than one of the stuffed greedy birds" didn't mean anything, what was she trying to say anyhow? Nothing mattered where everything mattered. Fuchsia sun-shade that caught the edge of a lapel of a coat and a flower pinned edgeways. The spray of lobelia-like blossom some one obviously off a boat (something he had snatched from a wall above a gondola) had stuck into his coat, caught colour and passed on fuchsia by way of the spray of – she had it – half opened dark wisteria, to the next bit of colour. Wisteria caught a blob of colour, thick Matisse paint blob from a bag lining, then the whole of a sprayed summer dress and artificial sweet-peas on a premature summer hat. Sweet-pea colour caught up the tassel on the tip of an erect parasol and from that … up, up to two women leaning out of an upper window. Above Florian's second doorway women peered across meagre leafage … the flowers might be petunias. Half-sensed intransient fragrance said "no … heliotrope." Smudge of colour in the window boxes … "I'm sure it's heliotrope."

Leaning above window-boxes, the shoulder of one woman let light strike across the amber features of the other. Light refracted and reflected through half-lit corridors apparently as in the day of Tintoretto, still exploited its odd bag of old tricks. "Those women up there, preening down, remind me of a balcony" (Raymonde shied off "heliotrope" as neither of them answered) "in Veronese." Say "Veronese" and you think "balcony" so she had said nothing remarkable, nothing to bring the angry colour back into Garry's cheeks and to make the eyes of Daniel go Book of Revelation's beryl or jasper or chrysoprase, one or all those colours, just for nothing, just for a change of thought, something that had automatically lifted the zinc shutter. Daniel's hands hung limp between his grey knees, his face was set straight like a face cut on a Hellenistic relief at (say) Ephesis. Ephesis. If you saw Daniel you couldn't get away from Greek things somehow, Garry was quite right. Garry saw in one dimension … outgrown trick of pre-war Raymonde's. Garry had inherited her outgrown Greek trick. "I did think Raymonde, when you wrote me, you would take the boat to Athens."

Garry was quite right, Athens was integrity, Athens was somehow Daniel. But Athens made a jagged line somehow across Raymonde's so suave contemplation. It cut spear-wise and silver flashed in this place of suavity, of colour, wisteria colour … she was reminded of wisteria above grey walls by a casual tourist. Wisteria, banners across walls, became violets of Athens etherealized, suave aura of reality. Garry was right … this was one remove, two removes from everything ... but it was true (Garry was wrong there) as the halo is as true, perhaps more true than the brow that wears it. Distant flowers scented the air ... as light, as ethereal as an aura ... "it *is* heliotrope." "What?" "That thing that vaguely scents things." Heliotrope in window boxes above Florian's second doorway again changed everything.

A word, a foot-step or a sea-wind fluttered banner ... waft of fresh scent, heliotrope in boxes, everything changed everything ... wisteria pulled off a wall in passing, stuck in an under-mannered tourist's coat flap ... the eyes of Miss Smithers from Newcastle-on-Tyne, Daniel who sat unmoved, yet fully sensed it. Raymonde had only to say "Veronese," "balcony" and she knew he saw what she saw. Hierograph ... beating in the air, dot and tick and tick and dot of super-sensuous language ... the fluttering of the streamers of the a-symmetrical symmetry of the lion banner, the tilt of a summer sun-shade, the fluttering of a pigeon ... everything means something, a candle on a candlestick, a bird pecking at a brioche ... heaven is getting things (thoughts, sensation) across in some subtle way, too subtle to grasp with intellectual comprehension ... this hieroglyph language she and Daniel had between them.

11

HIEROGLYPH LANGUAGE had beat in her room in London, things they hadn't said that she had from the first determined that they should not say. Gareth was right; say Daniel and you think Athens. Tall, with that odd light striking across his forehead, she had kept Daniel out of it, out of the book-shelf, out of the empty grate (it was summer) or the grate smouldering (it was autumn) or the wind beating down smoke, making her sophisticated little room seem a cottage room (it was early winter, she always stayed too late) in some sea-wind swept barren space of waters; sea and wind beating across London housetops. "I must be going soon now to d'y Vaud." Daniel was there, all the time and all the time she had pre-determined not to mix up Daniel with the furniture, with the beat and beat of countless outside matters, not to let emotion flood across and spoil the thing between them. Daniel had sat in her room pre-determined likewise, not to give in ...

... to things, people, all in odd disproportion, glazed effect of some bearded bull (Mordant wasn't bearded) and the red tiles and the blue tiles of some utterly inapposite set of values, some simple Kindergarten red-blue, blue-red palace made of bricks; bricks were set in such simple red-blue in some heavy temple, in some court across which Mordant padded in great flat sandals, tassels swinging somewhere, Zoroastering smatterings ... Anglo-Indian sort of atmosphere, hold on to that exact and precise falsity, "you must marry me," marry? Who, what and where was marry? And who and what was the thing looming up and up all dispropor-tionate? Alex Mordant had loomed heavy shouldered; he was not heavy. He was sturdy with that sort of physical directness of some great bull. Heavy trampling of great hooves might trample out the thing in her that burned and burned ... but the thing in her that burned and burned became like glass spikes under the great hooves of Mordant. "O, if you will be witty." "I wasn't on purpose, being witty." "If you will turn and catch a fellow up in every least particular." "I didn't, I wasn't. I only said that I didn't think you were quite right about Landor, that I don't think Shelly under-rated, that I do think something sometimes can yet be said for

Swinburne." Smattering of superficial criticism that made a little volume (his incredible poetry) turn and quiver under her hands and her desire to deceive him into thinking she could accept him become so great that she over-did it, said his metres were not in the least Miltonian, that the volume (printed by him privately in such delicate grey) deserved better at the hands of the *Quarter*, but everyone knew what the *Quarter* critics were like, what they were out for. "Tire not my love, weave grasses into chaplets" was not (the world knew what to expect of the *Quarter* critics) Spencerian by way of Francis Thompson. So anxious to make him think he was the more important that she leapt over, over the other side and instead of being trampled into numb obscurity, little glass spikes obtruded (why won't the gods let one just be trampled?) spiking little acrid pin points into his weighty ankles. Give up, give in. She had wanted Daniel to think she had given in to Mordant.

Katherine? Katherine didn't so much matter. Katherine was in the beat and slide of voices (Daniel's, Raymonde's) in their sliding off together, in their holding on together. Katherine didn't matter for they themselves exonerated and excused and negated and re-created Katherine in their every gesture. To talk about Katherine at all was to destroy her. To praise her was to negate her. They knew the thing she stood for. Katherine had shaped hieroglyph with them separately and now that they shared hieroglyph they were somehow sharing Katherine. Mystic language that they talked to-gether yet not knowing either of them (Raymonde, Daniel) until the very last that the other one had shared it. The terrible excite-ment of the thing kept her spiritually alive, she was certain, over that otherwise profitless season, kept her going, while she sustained herself, psychic vampire, on the quality of Mordant. Dragging up

Mordant, and image of this Mordant, in order to blind Daniel, to falsify herself, to satisfy herself that Daniel was unique, frigid, cold, remote and glacial. She used Mordant, as it were, furnace-red heat, to fix the brittle shape of Daniel. Daniel, brittle glass, became the more transparent, the more perfect in shape, in flawless contour, beside the thought of Mordant. "Yes, Mordant fascinates me. He is like a great bull," all the time the picture of Alex Mordant sustained her; she dragged it solemnly up, great captive bull (he too had come from Katherine) she needed this sacrificial thing between them, great bulk of remembered (in London) male body, heavy thighs, all the time drag up Mordant; does Daniel hate Mordant? Play the old game, priestess of some arcane cult, let's find out what hieroglyph is and let us get some colour of picture and written symbol into the air. Cold days (she had stayed on as usual too late in London) Daniel still came, and each time he came, she re-conjured in her little blue room this image of Mordant, to sustain her. Without that odd image of Alex Mordant, she never would have got through that odd preparation for initiation with Daniel. Hold fast to something, she had urged herself on, on, on with it, hold fast to Alex Mordant. "It isn't" (this in London) "that I want a lover. Not exactly want a lover ... Mordant is red flame of some sort of sacrificial poppies. Red and red. You know. Alex Mordant comes into this little room and sets it beating ..." "O quite ..." "I mean sets it beating. He comes into this room and there seem to be odd pyres, something Abyssinian, something of Asia Minor. He seems Zoroastrian ..." "O quite ..." "He seems like the priest of some cult of which I am ignorant, so something certainly not to do with intellect. It's obvious of course, you are Greek, Olympian. That's perhaps why you don't really so greatly interest me ... you know what I mean. Men have a way (the world accepts) of sinking with women to their lowest. Now with a mind, a sort of blade beating itself raw in your raw fore-head, a woman like myself must have some such like anodyne." "O yes ..." "It's nice of you to listen. I never talk to people. You see it was my pre-determination not to ... experiment ... that led me to this impasse. I know what it's all like ... I know what it all is. You are too high, too clear for me. You and I curiously don't belong together ..." "Curiously ..." "Now with Mordant ..."

Mordant had been red but curiously Mordant never had been Venice. Rome, late Rome had been in that gladiatorial bend of head on thick throat, in the lift of muscled arm, in the slight swagger of him, the bully and the inapposite delicate gracious way he had of speaking. Mordant was no poet, was no Greek; himself of some slight Anglo-Indian connection, some hint of battles and some red of battle-fields was something so alien, so unlike her, that Raymonde had turned to him last (was it only last?) summer before the appearance of this Daniel. Katherine (witch) had sent them both to see her. Mordant was red of some dripping gladiatorial sword blade ... "I like the rich quality of Mordant ..." all the time fascinated and somehow disappointed that she couldn't let go, that she couldn't let herself sink absolutely. "He has such a rare rich quality. There are actual fumes of reeking blood, pens in which cattle had trampled ... war and war is in the face of Mordant. Mordant is the last person in the world theoretically I would like..." she went on with it, on with it, beating back and back the persistent thing that had stared at her in London. Daniel had been white against her walls like that painting in the Scuolo ... he had been like a painting hung there, outwardly correct in all particular yet with his exact mondanity suggesting by some odd aura, some odd turn of head, other things, fine etched delicate Florentine frescoes, further back, perfect flawless reach upward of white throat on tall body, the turn, she could almost feel it, of fine collar bone under the grey or under the dark blue or under the fawn-brown of his shoulders. She had been so vivid, so certain of what had been there that there had seemed no reason for reaching across, drawing simply as one draws a curtain from before some holy statue, the cloth from those lean shoulders. Mordant was there too ... Mordant was there too. The moment her fingers were impelled, drawn almost magnetically across, to dynamo of that alert correct tall figure, she would drag back this thing, this Mordant like some sacrificial figure, some image set between them. Ghost to talk must have some sacrifice of red flesh ... ghosts to talk. She had led her thought, her words, systematically back to Mordant, Mordant so that the hieroglyph might remain between them.

Walls in her memory were shaking and drawing nearer, walls were shrinking and walls were receding; walls in London were about to crush them together like two bees in some fine scented stiff flower stuff of fragrant petal. Walls would recede, go on and on like little transparent boxes set one within another, geometric spider lines showing little box within little box ... hieroglyph. "I suppose it is wrong, but one knows, one feels people must have ... experience. Mordant that first day he called in early spring made me see blue tiles, he is Assyrian." Mordant had to be called in to glower before them. Walls receded, walls systematically contracted. Eyes had watched her like some eyes of hypnotizing Gorgon. Eyes set in that white face, zinc eyes ... when Greek meets ... when Greek meets ... "Of course it's obvious you are late Olympian. Too late for my predilection. Now with Mordant I suppose it was the hyacinths he brought me that made me think of blue tiles … blue tiles, red tiles, O it's *killing* … he writes poetry." "Anglo-Indian?" "Yes. Anglo-Indian. Everything rhymes with everything. He's trying to … to …" Her breath had caught her, she would choke over it "reform me. He thinks I write badly. I do, I do write badly …" her voice had flung high and high breaking that fine superimposed skeleton affair of little crystal boxes. Crystal boxes, would anything break crystal boxes? Daniel had stared and stared … when Greek meets … but he should know, he should see that she wasn't going to give in, give in to this thing. Something stared and stared in Daniel, zinc shuttered self that wouldn't let her see him. Well, he shall see me. He shall think this is me. Katherine would be sure to have taken pains to tell him some yarn, spin some Arachne web, some perfect Circe stuff about me. "Katherine said you … you …" his eyes widened. He waited to hear what Katherine said about him. "Katherine said you were a silver image with eyes of agate … with death … with death under your wings." Daniel had stared and stared, zinc shutter again shut in Daniel. "Now with Mordant … she's frightfully fond of Mordant."

STARING AND STARING in Saint Mark's Square … it was that middle werewolf officer who made her think of Mordant. She had forgotten Mordant. Mordant had served his purpose, sacrificial bull, slaughtered to make ghosts utter … ghost, white lily from Olympos … yet because Mordant had made this very ghost finally turn and finally bend before the rapture of her sustained negation, Mordant must remain (like those officers in the Square) part of her life, part of the thing that made her, part of the thing that saved her. No, not exactly saved her. It was Gareth who had saved her.

12

KATHERINE (WITCH) had set the whole thing going. Katherine having set the thing ablaze was yet powerless to quench it. Katherine started it, Gareth stopped it ... what had any one to do with anything? If Katherine hadn't started it, I wouldn't have met Daniel, if Gareth hadn't stopped it, I would have blazed out with Mordant. Katherine, Gareth, they were two antique coin sides, Katherine one side, towered head, some Asiatic goddess, many breasted, something monstrous that yet holds authenticity, Gareth the other side, boy Emperor, slightly undershot little chin that gave a baby frailty to the hard clear profile, clear fine line of profile, short hair and the boy-turn of chin and that frightening intensity; power, power and that tyrannical forceful head-line somehow negated by the child chin, child chin of some pre-Byzantine emperor, authentic but late, late Greek, Græco-Phoenician, my friends are all eclectic. Mordant was heavy trampling hoofs ... just red fire. Katherine had sent the whole thing spinning, triangle set on triangle that makes a star, the seal of Solomon, masonic middle west wears upon its watch chain. Seal of Solomon, masonic seal that middle west tourists in gondolas wear upon their watch chains. Reach up and grab at a tendril of wisteria ... it's all going on and on, "authenticity is in a middle west farmer grabbing at wisteria." "What?" "I said authenticity is in the middle west. I was thinking of a watch chain." "You're all over the place." "I know it. *You're* too perfect, You'll burst with your own perfection. Why don't you let go ever?" "I wouldn't let go in this place. It's positively evil." "You're wrong there." Katherine (witch) had set the whole thing going. Katherine was responsible for Gareth, Raymonde, Daniel sitting in little tin chairs, huddled slightly now that the sun was setting.

"We can't go on sitting in this shadow." Groups of chairs, still turned this way and that way as if ghosts were sitting on them, were left empty. Ghosts of parasols, ghosts of other parasols, all, all the many, many parasols, were furled, awnings were lifted, banners were somehow faded. Light struck a new note, a subtle harmony of things just about to fade out, colour was listless, ghost-colour, ghost wisteria. People had slipped off like ghosts slipping off while Raymonde had been thinking, while Raymonde had been quarrelling with Gareth. In proportion as the room in London had become real to her vibrant imagination, this somehow faded. Gareth is right sometimes. "Venice is somehow faded." Raymonde said "Venice is somehow faded" meaning it this time. Katherine was responsible.

Katherine had set the whole thing flying like a pin-wheel. Triangle on triangle that made a star, set flying. Sparks went off and off, sparks went off in London. What was left really but a bare skeleton of a star on a star? Rip star from star, Alex, Katherine, Raymonde, from star Gareth, Ray Bart, Daniel and you get clean star triangle and smouldered burnt out triangle. The triangle Raymonde, Daniel, Gareth was a sort of platinum-white self-luminous white thing, you couldn't dissipate it. Iron frame work of burnt out triangle of Katherine, Mordant, Raymonde being burnt out leaves residue of suffering. Gareth was insufferable.

What did Gareth know of the feeling of a burnt out frame work? What did Daniel? Alex Mordant knew things, Katherine was things. Why can't Gareth leave me alone to become something of the past? Just sink into things, part of a burnt out framework? Burnt out framework having performed its whirling function of trellis, so to speak, for flaming fire discs, yet *has* performed its function. Why can't Gareth leave me to be played out?

GARETH, RAYMONDE ... she was sick of Garethraymonde. She would have been done long since with Garethraymonde if it weren't for Daniel. Daniel was flicking his white fingers and the lame dove watched disconsolate from a distance for crumbs that didn't now fall. "Don't get another brioche. It's too late." If she didn't make some move, drag herself out of Florian's, Daniel would get more brioche. The waiter had swept the tray off ... Italians were ordering aperitif. There was a new mood at Florian's, the just before dinner aperitif glasses taking the place of tea things. Even sitting in Saint Mark's Square can't go on forever. She must get out of Florian's.

"You take Gareth. I'll come presently." She shot "you take Gareth" off suddenly, metallic voice that was not her voice. Her voice was not there, was shut up in walls that opened, in walls that receded. Wall shut her voice up like a bee in a flower petal. Flower petal on flower petal ... who says that London's dreary? In London there was a huge flower, her wee apartment, and her voice was shut in walls. Walls opened telescopically, walls receded. Microscope, telescope of little London room-walls, vision, her own vision was the living optical lens to a burnt out iron framework. I am only a lens, I'm really not a person. Gareth was staring at her.

Walls receded, walls opened. They were standing in Saint Mark's Square. Somewhere, somehow, someone (it must have been Daniel) had reached long thin hands down into grey cloth pockets, had dragged out lire, centesimi, little crumpled temporary looking bank notes. Change ringing on an emptied tea tray, change making a little clatter, smallest change left, small silver coin while Daniel swept up rumpled uneven little heaps of paper bank notes. Tiny notes, five or ten lire, a lire was just nothing, little oddment of assorted change left there for the waiter who was sweeping up little heap of tiny moneys into his brown lean fingers. Tea tray swept up, swish of cloth, he was already signalling to two remote slightly dazed Norwegian looking people, people off boats, boats kept coming, new arrivals, clothes dusty with travel, perhaps only from the day trip to Padua … Raymonde had been to Padua, long ago … in those days Italy was just Italy, now Italy was something … other. How was I to know when I told Gareth I would meet her that Italy had so changed? Italy had changed, rather I had developed feelers … in the old days I was a sort of Gareth who looked upon Italian art as Greek art gone rampant, dissipated. South Italy was bearable … being a part of Greece still. How was I to know that I'd grow awkward feelers?

Things, people, didn't exist now in any one dimension. How was I to know that Saint Mark's Square would hold so many different odd dimensions? She staggered slightly … laid hold on a steady chair back. She felt like a boat drifted, after peril, into a shallow hollow harbour. Saint Mark's Square was a hollow sheltered harbour. How could I realize how much suppression was blighting perception? How was I to know that I was going to love it? How was I going to know that I was going to love it … went on and on, a sort of tune beating synchromatically against Il Trovatore that had re-commenced opposite Aurora. Il Trovatore flung its challenge … its sort of sweetened bugle note … its call to sticky beauty. Say "Saint Mark's Square is a sort of a Turkish delight of beauty," say it emphatically as if you never loved it, say "Il Trovatore is the right music for such played out, breathed out beauty." Say all this with conviction, repeat, "I've been too long in Venice."

BEAUTY FLAMED after a moment of suspense, grey-dawn or grey twilight, some odd dimension ghost light that was the breath of Venice as it died before its ... resurrection. "Venice is played out," say rather "Venice was played out." For two minutes only, for a space of seconds only, for just as long as it had taken them to slide through little chairs turned sideways into the open space before the grouped chairs, Venice was played out. In just a second Venice was resurrected ... it was the lighting perhaps of various Windows, shop Windows, throwing ghost sun-light. Lights from Windows were like sun-light veiled with evening. A veil of dusk, veiled the shop light Windows. Venice rose from its bier ... being two minutes extinct.

Venice gone out like a flame in wind, is just as quickly lighted. I said "I've been too long in Venice." I said it with conviction, I'll reconcile Garry at any rate. I'll not let Garry suffer. "Venice is played out," and "Venice was played out" were both veils before a spirit. I want it so much that I'll go away to-morrow. "I understand, Gareth. We'll go away to-morrow."

13

DYNAMO OF comprehension that had whirred with such a pretty splutter was played out. Dynamo was a metallic burnt out frame of a thing.... Venice like Mordant, Raymonde, Katherine has gone out like a sizzling pin-wheel. Say "Venice has gone out" and say it with conviction for metallic voice had hurtled forth words from nowhere, words from some metallic fortress, words from Ray Bart. "I understand, Garry. We'll go away to-morrow." Raymonde, a burnt out framework, triangle on triangle stood facing Gareth in grey dawn-light. Dawn? "It isn't dawn, it's evening." "Dawn" she had said, not knowing that she said it. "It's not dawn ... it's evening." Garry was staring at her.

Garry was staring at her. Be decent, Raymonde. Garry sent you the wire, got you out of vibrant, weary, over-wrought loneliness and tension. Garry paid your fare here. You're the guest of Gareth. Be decent. You have behaved horribly. "Garry ... I'm awfully sorry." Say "Garry, I'm awfully sorry." Raymonde was too sorry to any more quite matter. Vibrant burnt out frame that had sizzled with dynamo vibration (the whole afternoon was one hectic dynamo vibration) still held frame work for a vision. I am nothing, a sort of lens at the end of a sort of telescopic, cannon-like, useless long tube. Iron and metallic burnt out residue ... of Freddie. Of Katherine. Of Mordant. I am nothing.

Garry was staring at her. "Do you mind Garry if I run along the arcade here and get one or two things? I told Marion I would find some leather for her ... or those awful bead things." Gareth was staring at her. Garry said "go on ... if you *must* buy things." Raymonde said before Gareth could say it, "I know they're simply awful. These awful old Christmas-tree sort of ornaments ..." dynamo had said "Saint Mark's Cathedral is a sort of Christmas-tree sort of cathedral." Burnt out dynamo now said "these awful bead things."

EYES REFUSED TO register things that wide eyes now saw. Window on window suddenly lighted as if from her own inner illumination. Venice isn't a dynamo any longer ... is surface on surface of light, things exist (Marco Polo existed) in it. Venice was shelf on shelf of varying sensation, shelf on shelf, each separate shelf set with its peculiar array of glassware, spiritualized Morello goblets, bowl and dishes, dark blue, blue green and that green that isn't there at all, the green like a surface of translucent water that you must assure yourself is there by moving this way, that way before an arcade window. Arcade vaulting, doorway to each arch, each arch a doorway to some specific kingdom ... "no, Daniel. I'll come later."

Daniel was staring at her but Daniel wasn't staring. "Where is Garry?" "She's waiting for me by the campanile. She doesn't like you going off alone this time of evening." "Garry hates all these tooled things. I wrote some people I'd find things. A girl I know – " she stumbled, "loved a portfolio I had ... you know. To keep her things in." "To keep her things in" meant specifically pages, typed pages, pages and pages. A portfolio seemed the only thing that mattered. Raymonde remembered a shabby worn portfolio. "I got one of these things ... years ago ... in Florence. A girl I know always wanted one just like it." Daniel was staring at her. "To keep her stuff in."

"To keep her stuff in" meant "to keep my stuff in," pages and pages re-written, over-worked, scrawled and re-typed and copied. Writing was no inspiration ... it was pages and pages and some-times one got out of oneself because one wrote, people did things. "Garry liked my writing." Say "Garry liked my writing," what did it mean? It meant, Garry paid my fare here and I have behaved outrageously. "Garry paid my fare here." Daniel said "Gareth has a new plan." It didn't matter about Gareth and her new plan, it didn't matter about Daniel standing in the arcade before Morello goblets, it didn't matter that Gareth had a new plan. "Don't, don't keep Gareth waiting." Gareth was waiting alone by the campanile, hating Venice, hating Italians. "I have to do some shopping if I'm going. Tell Garry that I'll be back ... in half an hour. I'll be back and do the packing. Tell Gareth that I'll be back, tell Gareth I'll be packing." Dynamo was burnt out ... at the end of a burnt out iron frame or long cannon tube or framework, was a glass lens. All that mattered was looking at Morello goblets in a lighted window.

LIGHT CAUGHT LIGHT from light, the upslope of a green Morello goblet gave back dynamic highlight from the underside of a flat dish on the glass shelf above it. Light on a minute uplifted arm of a minute tall marble goddess repeated its reflection across the rounded marble head of a miniature discobolus. Windows reflected windows and the arches were repeated in bright surface of morocco, in gilt leather surface and fine surface broken by delicate inset gold leaf, tiny conventionalized tulip or rose pattern of more formalized Florentine leather. Leather, glass, beads; beads, glass, leather beyond Florian's little open partitioned porticoes and windows the other side of Florian's, leather, beads, beads, leather were hung outside windows that held marble discobolus, little minute goddess with uplifted minute forearm, so delicate, one flick of finger would break tiny replica of Praxitilean forearm. Books, books, books. Exquisite binding, leather again, leather with odd occasional lapse of taste, atrocious taste, leather inset like the stone inset on the front of the cathedral, atrocious taste blurred here into the general perfection of the whole thing so that you could not say, this is terrible, this glass dolphin with goggle-eyes peering so ludicrous and exaggerated is bad taste carried to its logical conclusion or this or this or this particular shelf of tooled leather is so much worse than that particular shelf or this string of beads is preposterous, for beads caught light, leather caught light, uplifted forearm caught light and gave it back in varying dimension … Daniel was standing by her.

Daniel was standing by her. How long had he been standing? "These awful, awful bead things." Say again "these awful bead things," indicating bunches of beads hung outside windows like ropes of pearls. Glass beads were priceless pearls, all of Venice was priceless. Glass beads were under-water, deep-sea plunder, things collected by these odd sea creatures; anemone coloured beads were blobs of closed anemones. "Glass beads are so atrocious."

"Are they?" Daniel was looking at her. He was standing, tall neophyte's wand, the just so far, no further. Hat tilted a little forward, stick over one grey arm. "Don't, don't keep Garry waiting."

SHE WOULD PLUNGE forward (now Daniel had gone), become part of these things; individuality didn't matter, people mattered. He who loses his soul shall save it ... soul flung away like a single pearl returned in highlights on glass goblets. Light caught light and Venice never had been lovelier. She was tenuous in it, underwater sea-grass, reaching out under-water" sea-feelers that must encompass all this. Snail on the slippery glass outside of a glass aquarium ... she was embodied having done with water-feelers and was as highly involved as a snail with protective shell in addition to long feelers. Gareth is a snail that won't stick out its feelers ... small horn-feelers like a butterfly. I am greater than sea-grass having defined intention. I crawl up this glass pane like a snail inside or outside a square aquarium glass tank, filled, as it happens with Morello goblets. Light caught light (she passed to the next window), leather work again, not such atrocious bad taste. I should go in here ... one grey Morello goblet was set like a chalice on a square of velvet. Wine-coloured velvet rumpled across a glass shelf ... one goblet set upon it.

Grey glass ... that goblet must be grey glass. If I go in and buy that goblet I shall hold the soul of Venice. I shall own Venice as King Canute owned England. I shall lose Venice as Canute ... lost. Back O back thou foaming brine. Venice crept up, receded, crept nearer, retrogressed, drawing her further with it. I am hypnotized by Venice. Garry hypnotized me, Daniel hypnotizes me. I evade personal hypnotic eyes through these eyes. Venice is all eyes, a pattern on a bird wing. I have escaped … have I escaped? Eyes are the colour of that smoke grey, of that pearl grey. Grey with the texture of water, of dew before sunrise, of dew on a grey over-cast morning. The grey of water before the sun rises, these Venetians are diabolic, who would ever think grey glass could be so beautiful? It is the grey of the intelligence of grey eyes. It radiates intelligence, the light that is spirit, that is matter, that is Daniel. Daniel in London was just some such colourless fine glass … Mordant had made him fine glass. Raymonde in her determination to keep hieroglyph between them had kept him fine glass. How long can I stand here staring?

LIGHT CAUGHT LIGHT in varying dimension. New windows cast new squares of light and broken oblong of light fell across her shoulders, across shoulders of passengers off boats (loitering like herself before windows) before blue-grey Italian shoulders, small sturdy men, now a very lean one, bald, that lean one with his cap off looks age-old with his cap off, young chin thrust forward with his cap on again, his hand running along his sword-hilt.

Aurora was playing lustily again across the street and now in the open the swarm of foot passengers from under the Clock Tower pushed and swarmed, black river suddenly debouching into the lamp-lit open space before Saint Mark's Cathedral. Clock above her head, ding-ding, loud, then in a moment, there would be the answering ding-ding (seven times was it?) from the other odd (in Venice) Germanic figure of a bronze Gaul. Clock with figure of Scorpio, Balance, Twins. The signs of the Zodiac made a sort of coronal at the feet of the Madonna. Why can't Gareth see the joke the place is?

Swarm of black and grey, men mostly, soldiers with pleasant feathers upright in grey forester-like soft hats pulled sideways, the sort of hat Rosalind would wear in a school play, soldiers swaggering across the square, Orlandos and Mercutios. Why can't Gareth see the joke? Cathedral emitting an aura, a sort of mesh to enclose, to drag one in, to pull one in. It's true the place is dangerous, Garry says the place is dangerous ... this reaching out of aura to pull one in, in, to drag one in, in ... great flower, Saint Mark's Cathedral showed apertures in great flower. Pulling her in, pulling her in ... she entered by the little further side door, she had staggered past the first door, "I won't go in." She had staggered past the great central door with her foot pausing a moment on that very flag stone she had so eloquently held forth on, over brioche, Austrian bomb that never killed a pigeon, staggered past valiantly, turned tail and slid surreptitiously into the little furthest door ... just why is it Gareth hates Cathedrals?

Cathedral, church, temple. If you called this thing a temple then Gareth would adore it. This thing is a temple. Raymonde slid into grey. She slid from intersecting light on light, light from the Mercato broken with its swarm of foot-passengers, light from Aurora and Florian and light breaking across light in her avid brain, striking reflection from glass on a glass shelf or the rounded poised head of a minute Discobolus. If a tiny discobolus were placed in that empty niche and this were Byzantium, Gareth would say the thing was beautiful. Light across light in her tired brain. The cool slightly fragrant corridor rose, flooding her like water.

"We float like water, into water, float into some luminous state between us. Gareth is like water. Daniel is pure water. Water gone arid is dangerous. I drink Gareth like water and Gareth is tainted water." She had stooped to drink at a clear well-head and had shuddered back at the realization that the source was tainted. She drank in Gareth, had imbibed Gareth, intellectual sustenance for so long, it seemed incredible that Gareth should be tainted. Gareth is always right. Gareth is never right. Gareth is absolutely right, was absolutely right in her perception about Mordant. Gareth was quite, quite wrong in her perception about Mordant. Gareth hates Saint Mark's Cathedral, therefore Gareth is somehow tainted. Something has tainted Gareth. Call it some phobia if you will. I'm tired of Gareth's phobia. Gareth's phobia is a python rising in the loveliest surroundings to terrify me, to drag me back, back to my own forgotten terrors. Gareth has no right to terrorize.

Hysteria was through and around them. The whole fault is Gareth's. There is no fault in Gareth. Gareth is the purest thing I have ever yet encountered. She is tight and eastern, a lotus-bud. She is a child Buddha seated on a leaf regarding a spread lotus flower. Gareth is perfect and Gareth is perfection. There is a kind of perfection that turns devilish. Gareth is perfection turned a devil. How dared Gareth shudder yesterday (was it yesterday?) before the Tintoretto? Christ looks to John, young God with his friend, Christ and John, lover and lover God and God, young Helios with his friend, Hyacinth … Mordant brought me those blue hyacinths. How Gareth hated Mordant.

The room, the London room where Gareth hated Mordant enclosed her, so that crouched now on the little wooden bench set against the far wall, far and far in the dimness of the cathedral inner door-way, Raymonde was in her own room, facing Gareth across blue hyacinths … "but I tell you he is evil." "How can you know a thing is evil that you never yet saw? You haven't and you won't meet Alex Mordant. How can you say so absolutely that Alex Mordant is evil when you never saw him?" "I feel him … I know when he comes to see you. The whole place reeks of Mordant." "You don't know when he comes to see me. You know he's been by the flowers. You can't say Mordant's evil." "I know anyone having anything however remotely to do with – with Katherine is perverted. I know that Mordant came from Katherine." "You know that Daniel came from Katherine." "Daniel is different. Daniel is something different" … hysteria in Raymonde's luminous brain roused its head, rose to confront her in the cool slightly fragrant darkness. A light was burning in the distance in the slightly fragrant darkness … pillars loomed, cut across by faint gold. Peering with concentrated attention, eyes peering upward like a water beetle from the depths of dark cool water, Raymonde perceived that the gilt, like tilted flower heads, was letters, faded letters, Maria in faded gilt Greek letters. Christos written in faded letters like the letters on the hyacinth. God, Theos, God, Greek for God, Greek God was written in faded Greek letters. Her mind, a lily, rising on tall stem rose out of confusion, out of hysteria … Gareth is quite wrong. This place is beautiful. To say "this place is evil," is to confuse beauty with destructiveness. Gareth's phobia is not Gareth. How to break Gareth from her phobia?

14

HER MIND, a lily, rising on tall stem, rose out of confusion, out of hysteria … loss of identity she had found this afternoon (among amber sunlit spaces and amber shadow and sun-shades like so many brilliant lotus lilies) is the gift of Venice. Occult gift of the Marco Polo orient, loss of identity. Loss of identity is the gift of Venice, power to crawl, snail self up the surface of high window and creep half-hatched moth in among tenuous rootlets and dynamic deep earth feelers. Her mind, a lily, rising on tall stem, rose out of confusion, out of hysteria ... Daniel was sitting by her. How long had he been sitting?

"I've been praying, thinking." "It's the same thing" ... She did not have to say "look at this drinking fountain." Daniel was staring at it. The fountain shone, polished agate, enormous agate cup, marble baptismal fountain that had stood filled with water, perhaps with a jet of running water in the hall of some Tiberius – "I mean, this baptismal fountain – " in the depth of a great hall; Saint Mark's columns rising out of dimness were in truth portals of the house of some high deity. Tiberius, Zeus, Jehova. God had built from man's bed-rock of leavings. "This thing expresses everything. The whole renaissance is in this drinking fountain." Baptismal fountain was upheld by dancing cherubs. Dolphins were ringed beneath it.

The footsteps of people, tourists, priests, all alike at home here ceasing suddenly, left them alone in some familiar hall-way. They were seated, it was obvious, in the atrium of a palace. When Greek meets, appositely, Greek ... it was obvious Greeks talk hieroglyph. "Look at the drinking fountain" meant "and how is Garry?" Daniel knew that the "whole renaissance is in this drinking fountain" meant "I am worried about Garry." The mind, a lily, rising on tall stem, rose out of confusion, out of hysteria ... "I loved her ... terribly."

"I mean," a voice continued, her voice? "I have loved ... terribly. It's terrible to love and know oneself inadequate and helpless." "So she says." "So – ?" "Gareth. She says she is sorry for me if ... I love ... Ray Bart." "Being sorry does no good to any one. I am sorry for myself, harassed and lacerated loving ... Daniel." Sparks were drawn into one tall light. One candle burned where inappositely darkness had made cornice and square mosaic shine like goldfish. Mosaic, now candle light had dimmed it, she realized, had been glittering goldfish. "I never noticed till this year that all mosaics, even the most banal here, have a sort of fervour. They glint and glow in the dusk like goldfish in grey water. I've been watching."

INAPPOSITE TURN of wrist that candle light showed was turned from a master chisel, made Raymonde say "I had enough of Greek things. I said I wanted something … so-called Christian mysticism that finds complete co-relation with so-called classicism. I have found it this time and with you, in Venice. I never really understood, accepted the renaissance till this time." Turn of wrist that eyes fastened on (her own?) grey eyes, harpy eyes like Katherine's. "Katherine and I were happy. We talked, gouged each other's souls out. You know how it was with Katherine." "O quite …" "I mean Katherine made it possible to accept … Gareth. Without Katherine there had been no Gareth. Without Gareth, there had been no … Daniel. I don't know what's the matter…." Mind rising like a lily, looked and saw the whole thing. "We're not three separate people. We're just one."

Ghosts to talk must have some sacrifice of red flesh … she had realized, phrased exact image, seen clearly. Now seated in Saint Mark's Cathedral toward the midish lateness of an early evening, Raymonde was again reminded … people, things don't exist in themselves unless you, suave dynamo of apprehension, are there to re-create them. Daniel it was evident never had existed. Now Daniel was existing.

"Gareth is secular, clerical, a mechanical little wound-up little clock work. Her heart is where her brain is." Say "her heart is where her brain is," it means "my heart is where my brain is …" Say "my heart is where my brain is" realizing that flash on Morse-code flash of mosaic above (now) a triple row of candles wouldn't be there for the heart to bow to if the brain, suave dynamo, were not there to receive it. Vibration reaches apposite vibration. Daniel was sitting by her.

Vibration that reaches, twists a little, shrapnel to cut soul neatly from a weary nerve racked body, that was Katherine. Vibration carefully attuned, little machine to catch, tick tick of mechanically perfect telegrammatic centre, that was Gareth. "Gareth is purely mechanical in all her reaction." "Purely?" "Well ... not quite." There was, it was apparent, a catch somewhere. "You know what I mean, she sees me rather than perceives me." "How can that make the difference?" "She watches me ... watching. She doesn't want to watch me absorbing. She wants to watch me watching." Glitter of triple row of candles set before madonna were so many leaping fire-flies. How could anyone leave Venice?

IF DANIEL SAID "I love you" there would be obstructing matter. There would be red and red, cardinal red, the red of Freddie Ransome. If Daniel said "I love you" there would be red of countless un-named sort of people, the red, red, red of un-remembered legions, "Caesar. I mean Tiberius or Caesar. Countries, Germany, England are it is apparent (or were) Roman." The candles went on flickering. This obviously was Athens.

"I mean this is, isn't it pure Greek? I mean this is, isn't it; the last of the last of the last of the tide wave of Greek beauty?" Saint Mark's Cathedral seemed to her apprehension now to be what it always had been. In text books one had been wont to read "Byzantine art reaches its climax in the Adriatic." Byzantine art of text books was Greek art. The wave washed across the islands, *lily on lily that o'er lace the sea* to Asia Minor. Inappositely somehow finding a scant foothold on a half Asiatic sea board, the wave flowed backward. The wave, flowing backward, flowed again forward. "Byzantine art finds its last, its subtlest expression here in Venice."

Say "Byzantine art finds expression," all things from an old text book. Say Byzantine art and that meant the back wash of the Greek-Rome that was Byzance. Bubbles set on Roman foundation, a Greek comment (says the text book) of Greek on Roman architecture, Byzance. The queen of the Adriatic held her treasure ... it was Athens.

Tiberius outer hall-way held two pale Greeks ... "I should so like to hate her."

WHEN GREEK MEETS ... it was obvious they so seldom did meet that arches had to be placed on arches, stone on stone. Men, architects from across two oceans had to fetch Lybian limestone, had to bring basalt from Assyria, had to plunder ancient temples for just this red stone. Red stone fitted into green stone, stalactites were a little twisted to form columns that upheld other columns. When Greeks meet ... had to be prepared for. Just such a meeting had long since been predicted. Candles flickering in diminishing twin rows showed goldfish mosaic. Christos was written in Greek letters, Maria, Theos. God was written in Greek letters for this moment. "I meant hating would mean consummate expression, to hate and to hate. To hate Gareth you see is to hate my own brain." Her own brain now was static, cloud of outward circumstance had so contrived it. Her own mind rising, a lily on tall stem out of hysteria, examined carefully *loss of identity is the gift of Venice*, "Crystalized and over static identity ..." she stumbled. Words when Greek meets Greek mean nothing. "You crystalize identity."

"I always do have a queer effect on people." "I should think so. So Katherine told me." Her heart which had a moment since been root fibre and tentacle and outreaching subtle sympathies, now almost palpably seemed elsewhere. Her heart which had spread wide, wide, many tentacled sea-anemone, now closed fast. Her heart was a red drop of stale blood. "O Katherine …"

"To love and to love and to love … was the gift of Katherine." "To hate rather…" "To hate and to hate and to hate … was the gift of Katherine." Katherine had been (in London) in the slide of their two voices, in their speaking, in their non-speaking. "She tampered with things." "O quite …" "With you palpably." Head bent forward was head of young Sebastian. Head bent forward had been head of seated Hermes. "She gives and … takes. She is the Trojan mistress, Cassandra left forsaken. Light, the manifold Theos, Greek for God, for Helios, left Katherine … left Cassandra. Cassandra shouting at a crossroad … that is Katherine." Saying all that, she thought, if it weren't for Katherine, where were hieroglyph between us? Then someone said "Katherine is the only person in the world who ever really loved me."

Daniel had just said "Katherine is the only person in the world who ever really loved me." How could that be true? To see Daniel was to see beauty. Beauty a narthex, the neophyte's wand, then was utterly rejected? How could one say, how could one ever have said "Daniel you are beauty." Daniel was so obviously beauty, had been, that it were waste to say it. Is it possible that hieroglyph never had been between them?

Theos god for Greek, Greek god is written in Saint Mark's Cathedral. If you want to worship Greek for God and Greek god you may do in Saint Mark's Square. Greek for god sat patiently beside her. Was it possible that Daniel didn't know he was that?

A shell and a ball of light, a snail crawling on a window … a mind reaching out and out, perceiving and apperceiving … soul tentacles stretched to their furthest like a harp wire breaking, was it possible it all meant … nothing? Her mind, a lily on tall stem, rose out of confusion, out of hysteria … her heart was where her mind was. "Little crystal boxes are all somehow breaking somewhere." Daniel said "O quite.…"

WAS IT POSSIBLE little crystal boxes then meant simply nothing? That holding on and saying in a little bee in a flower room in London, "Daniel is simply perfect" to oneself, never committing oneself to that thing outright, had meant valour sustained for nothing? Is it possible that hieroglyph of "Katherine is always innate when it comes to outright vision, oracle manqué, she is a vision manqué" had meant nothing? Was it possible that sliding down a steep incline, a sort of undignified spiritual sleight of hand, sort of bob-sled on a tea-tray, the sort of talk with Mordant had meant nothing? Was it possible that "Gareth is unhappy" that "Byzance is Greek comment on Roman architecture" had meant nothing? Is it possible that all the time and all the time, shut up in crystal boxes had meant nothing? Was it possible that Daniel was a sort of long drawn out little boy, like a tall long drawn out little boy who sees himself long and drawn out, tenuous in water? Is it possible that Daniel was only Daniel seen in water?

Candles went on. More candles sprung up where old candles wilted. Bee drones were droning in a sort of bee-hive at the half broken off far end of the far Cathedral. Floor sagged under her feet, mosaic sinking downward as mosaic in Saint Mark's Cathedral always had done. "It's odd thinking of this floor flooded, isn't it? Garry was telling me that when she was a child she came here ... the very Cathedral floor was under water." Was it possible that hieroglyph of reading newspaper headlines (thousands of dial-turns back) about the fallen campanile had meant nothing? Daniel, it was apparent, was hardly born when the campanile fell down. Venice flooded ... campanile fallen ... people, things existing in dial surface, back and back and a dial-turn further back than anyone can remember. "I remember how shocked my mother was when the campanile fell down ..." years and years and years went back, a dial hand spinning backward. "They loved Venice."

"They loved Venice" was hieroglyph of another order. "They" was people who lived out of time, out of space, a sort of spiritual sifting of fine values, the sort of sifting of values and finding Daniel seated there beside one, like a drawn-out little over-weedy little brother. Brothers, husbands, people like that ... was the sacrifice then nothing? "Brothers, husbands ..." Raymonde began to Daniel. What was a brother, anybody's brother, but a forgotten relic? People had forgotten what brothers, husbands had done. People were forgetting. There was the after-math, the Gareth-Robins. "Is Gareth worried do you think? Does Garry worry do you think about poor Robin Rockway?"

BROTHERS, HUSBANDS, Robin Rockway spiritually winged, made one see that hieroglyph was nothing. Daniel was somehow (how would it be possible?) the one thing untainted. Red lilies, cardinal red, doge red, the red of morning day-flowers, the brilliant tiger lily. Saint Mark's Cathedral was so many hollow lilies, some placed edgewise ... bees crawl into martagons, into Turks-cap lilies. A yellow lily opened ... it was her room in London.

"I go back, Daniel seeing my room in London. I'm afraid I didn't help you." Daniel was sitting by her. There was a scale of values outside the crystal boxes, outside the cerebral intensity that reached out, weed-fibres, into anybody's garden. There was herself shut up in crystal boxes and there was herself that crawled, a snail, outside a window. Snail outside a window had escaped Gareth. Self in crystal boxes in a little room in London had got away from Daniel. "All I wanted … was to get away … from people."

Spiritual values shifting means little boxes breaking. Would anyone in the whole world know what it meant to say (she was saying it) "that curious feeling that I've been here … it's easy to explain it. My mother came here …" How to go on now that one had started, knowing that pre-natal influence must mean something, that things happened before things happened, that things were always happening? Daniel was a little boy drawn out and out and out. Daniel was unprotected. Daniel must be protected. Daniel was herself drawn out like herself in water. Daniel in a little London room was herself drawn out in water. Room went vague in her head and room … like crystal breaking … made odd comment on things her tears were. Tears falling are crystal boxes breaking. "I never cry. I'm sorry."

If Daniel said "I love you," Daniel would be calling red sacrifice from quiet clods of dark earth. Red sacrifice was red sacrifice. Red sacrifice had become drab, had then been forgotten. All the time while there was sacrifice and sacrifice, Daniel was waiting for this. For a moment in Saint Mark's Square when there would be no wall of little boxes … she said "Gareth is waiting for us." Is Gareth waiting for us? All the time Daniel was a little boy, then a child drawn out tenuous and overgrown, then herself simply seen like her own self seen in water. Daniel was waiting, a small long drawn out small thing grown over long and tenuous. When the campanile fell, Daniel was not grown … Daniel was now grown. "You'll take care of Gareth for me."

TO SAY "YOU'LL take care of Gareth for me" was a twisted way of saying "you'll take care of me for me." Courage ebbed out, seeing the wall was static. Lily rose out of confusion, hysteria was static. "It's good to have a real cry." Her handkerchief twisted to a hard knot really showed the cry was not real, it was the squeak that doors sometimes make in opening, that doors will make in shutting. Tears and the sort of hard little gasp that went with that sort of crying were simply hinges screeching. She hadn't had her cry out. She wouldn't have her cry out. Cryptic two-sided Delphi was weighing the whole matter. "I suppose Katherine kept you for me."

"I suppose Katherine kept you for me" meant "I suppose Katherine kept me for me." They were a sort of monster. "We have one eye between us." "One – ?" "Eye. We're like that Gorgon monster. I mean the monster Perseus met going to meet the Gorgon. They had one eye between them."

Something, Helios, Perseus, light anyway incarnate was going to slay a monster. He needed their eye. I see, Gareth sees, Daniel sees. We rise to some height of vision and are as quickly blinded. We see too far seeing nothing. Something outside all racial scale of values, that was Greek so simply, was waiting to slay a monster. Thought, ambition were all designed for one thing. Keep yourself alert for the moment when it's your turn. Together they were all things, separated they were nothing. Take it, even, that one of the three of the odd claimants got the whole eye. That one would be lost in the world of super-vision without one or the other of the other two to guide it. Daniel was lost in the world ... and so was Raymonde. It was obvious that somehow there was some catch. "Have we hogged the eye between us?"

Daniel said "what?" turning sharply toward her. "What hogging what between us?" He was questioning as Garry had been. Daniel watched her thought glint and vanish as Garry always would do. Her thought had a way of flicking bright sort of snake-tail while the snake head was elsewhere. Daniel waited for the thought head to re-emerge and sting him. He thought something was going to sting him … he saw … tears were a door that's squeaking. "I mean you and I, have we in some odd way, intending not to do it, managed horribly to hurt Garry?"

15

IF A DOOR opened, a door shut. Barometerized blue blotting paper, I go, you come. Little bells in the vault above her beat their bell notes. Outside, booming like a thunder cloud of wild bees, more and more bees (bells) were burrowing into (she supposed) shafts now of brilliant moonlight. Sound like bees she was certain was now cutting across silver moonlight like wasps across white poplars. Bark of poplar trees, moonlight shining, the intolerable white of Greek light. The Greek was intractable, spiritual tyrant. Her mind a lily, rising out of hysteria, saw things clearly. Love and love and love are something other. Something transcending love and love was the gift alike of Greek and Jewish prophet … "we'd best get back to Gareth."

Daniel, soul sperm, yeast or leaven was thrown out, it was obvious after the perished Freddie Ransomes and surviving Mordants. Wasn't she exactly like everyone when Daniel faced her? Or more exactly when she was faced with Daniel? She was afraid of Daniel. Regarding now a Daniel with still half-frozen features marring and destroying the drug and oriental peace of that cathedral's odd interior, Raymonde (tall lily rising on stem) was faced with ardent issues. Mordant, Katherine were a coin tossed upwards. Coin fell, it was obvious with a pretty mantic clatter … Gareth, Daniel faced her. "I'm thinking still of Gareth." "Gareth is waiting for us." "I know … I knew all the time." "She sent me here to find you." "I know … I knew she would do." "I knew where I would find you." Things like that didn't need to be said between them. They shared one eye between them.

Soldiering was ugly, had defeated its own purpose. You can't go back, go back to Alex Mordant. Soldiering was ugly … with soldiering was beauty. You can't go back, having gone starkly through it, to exactly that … Beauty with War for lover. Ares and achievement. Achievement of that sort wasn't worth the having. But you had to have it. Stars shone above ravished war fields. So Daniel.

"I have understood better than I ever have done … these things." Her hand, tall lily rising out of darkness, was something she watched cutting the air before her. Her own hand, symbol of her now firm crystallized intention, ploughed through air that was spiced with acrid tonic sweetness. Fumes drifting from a far altar were the incense fumes Simon the (was it?) Cyrenian had laid at a shut portal. Gates shut, gates opened, Christ, Janus-faced like the deity of Delphi, was keeper of shut portals. Portals were closed … they had been dead completely. Everyone was dead (not only brothers, husbands) had been for space of a many arid winters. Stars shone, were shining above battles. "I mean it's been going on all this time. We sit in a tomb with Mary. The tomb has been spread with symbol, cryptic letter. Look, there is symbol, cryptic row of letters." Christos in Greek, Theos, God in Greek and Mary. Christos, the light was waiting, Mary robed in blue who was everybody's mother. Hand on neophyte's rod or narthex. I am their sort of mother.

"I mean I wanted to get things across through Gareth. She stood there, a sort of silver dam across a flowing river. Robin Rockway leapt barriers, leapt the river, is lost, no irrigation stream (intellectual leaven) in him. I waited, champing, chafing at firm banks. Garry is a firm bank." Raymonde knew now facing Daniel, that Garry wasn't now that. "I have got away from my claustrophobia by coming here to Venice. I found I could get out, get away ... but it was leaping barriers. I found I could break (almost) Gareth. But that was Robin's method. With you ... I found a new sort of method."

BUT WHAT DID method matter? What did anything matter? Tall lily rose, mind facing stranger issues. "You see, I believe ... in you." "Katherine is the only person who really ever really loved me" might have its counter coin side. "Katherine is the only person who ever really loved me" meant a shattered Daniel shut up in crystal boxes. Loving and loving was the gift of Katherine, they had been Adon gardens, both of them brought to swift premature psychic flowering. Katherine had nipped (had had all intention to nip) the bloom off. Flowers had been there (for both of them) adequately protected. Little crystal boxes formed conservatory glass for Adon premature swift flowerings. They had both been protected. "There comes a moment when protection's no use. It kills one."

There was this new protection, this going into all things ... but it wouldn't do for Gareth. Gareth was protected by little iron scales of sheer intellectual plate mail. That was and wasn't (was it?) crystal boxes. Garry was small bee-visaged, sort of astral coloured angel. "Garry is a bee-winged small sort of astral-coloured angel."

"We live in both worlds, don't we?" There was patent danger in this. Living in crystal boxes, it was obvious spelt danger, getting quite out spelt danger. There must be a sort of balance. Daniel was staring at her. She knew why people loathed him.

"You hurt horribly."

FLING ACID, base into a crystal test tube … watch and watch things sizzle. So said the eyes of Daniel. Daniel's eyes were flooded with Daniel's eyes, black flooded across ice grey, pupils synthesized to darkness gleaned across fumes in a dead sepulchre. Daniel was staring at her. How long had he been staring? Turn clock dial back and back to last year, to that year I married Ransome to years and years back till you came to Katherine. Daniel was a tall child, was a flowering weed in water. Back and back and people said "the campanile's fallen" or "Saint Mark's Cathedral's flooded … danger to Saint Mark's Cathedral," and still Daniel's eyes were watching. Psychic pre-natal thought had moulded Daniel. Herself had moulded Daniel. Venice was in her, before ever she was yet born, my mother loved it; dial hand went swiftly backward, my mother came to Venice on her honeymoon, a small child boasting to other children. Small child paper doll distinctions. Where did *yours* go? Honeymoons make children … so this psychic pre-natal sort of loving. I loved Daniel all the time, all the time Daniel waited … I was a sort of psychic mother all the time to Daniel. Katherine who would have marred him sent him to me. It was the act of Delphi.

"People hate you, it's now quite obvious, Daniel." His eyes went on watching things sizzle and rush round in test tubes. Things inside Raymonde went rushing round in test tubes. Keep yourself stark, be yourself a sort of test tube. Could Daniel know how horribly he hurt her? Daniel is looking at me. I won't fail him. I hate Daniel looking at me … when Greek meets … *Greek* something is bound to happen. No one else was ever quite that … Freddie was sort of

Dionysus, a sort of affable acceptance. Mordant was like that. Mind concedes place to sheer physical ecstasy ... yet stands on guard, still armour plated outside. Athene could admit a Dionysus at the feet of the Acropolis. This is no separation of self into little boxes, Athene and Dionysus who was no more than cyclamen light on silver. This is not that. This is equality ... when Greek meets *Greek*. Daniel would like to break me. Daniel won't have me broken, he's too interested in test tubes. "I know why people hate you."

"People hate you for the same reason that they hate me, Daniel."

You give your soul to one thing, you can't give it to another. Yet is that true? She had given her soul to abstraction, little crystal boxes, she had given her soul to loss of identity, a snail outside an aquarium sort of window. Soul putting out feelers was lost without crystal boxes to confine it ... soul shut in crystal boxes too long and too deliberately is in psychic danger. Daniel was, had been, in psychic danger. For the sake of some self, *my* self, she hadn't reached out to Daniel. In London it had been "Katherine is oracle manqué," pure hieroglyph between them.

Katherine, Delphic projection, wouldn't be negated. Katherine had sent them to her. Mordant opened war-sealed physically vibrant areas, Daniel linked her up to Gareth. If I had broken from Daniel I would have negated Gareth. They were a set of planets revolving round and round and round a central fixed intention. Intention pre-established, cryptic, smiling. Intention said, I lie upon incense clouded tomb slab, I lie in a shut up cathedral. Claustrophobia of Christianity. Gareth was afraid of Saint Mark's Cathedral because it was (as seemed hieratically fitting) a fine carved and exquisite tomb for the body of a spirit. Weren't all cathedrals when they reached their occult high water mark just that? Crawl into Saint Mark's Cathedral like a bee into a furled flower head. Crawl in like a lobster into a lobster pot not wanting to get out ever.

"Garry hates this because it is a sort of, sort of ... denial ... not that ... you know what I would say, sort of negation of the spirit." By negation of the spirit she knew she meant negation of the thing in crystal boxes. "I mean negation of her spirit." If you are that, you have to be that. Gareth was true to her gun-metal standards. "Gareth is true to standards." Raymonde knew that Gareth was true, that Daniel was true, it was herself had failed them. "I know I failed her. She would never have been angry." Numbing drone of great bees in the distance. "I want to be a great bee."

"I want to crawl in and forget everything in this thing." Slim intellectual wand bearer, herself narthekophoros, she regarded (seated still as he had been all this time) Hermes-Sebastian. Hermes-Sebastian smiled his cryptic two sided smile. "You are Hermes and Sebastian."

Saint Sebastian pierced full of arrows, smiling and numbed, self-hypnotized, valour of pure spirit, or pure mind in spirit that gilds itself with some hypnotic power. Or rather silvers itself over. Daniel's mind had the power of silvering over Daniel. He shone as if in armour, himself armour bearer and the slim thing beneath it. He said "you have the tortured silly smile of some archaic statue." "I know." "Rather tight. Looking mincing almost." "I know." "You don't know, I'm rather glad you don't know." "Why – why glad Daniel?" "It's – *horrible.*"

When Greek meets Greek ... in Saint Mark's Cathedral ... it's something that's prepared for. Something all the time when Lybian deserts had been searched for this red stone and this blob of lapis lazuli and this knot of emeralds that bulges above the cross set in with sapphires on the over-ornate late Byzantine little shutter be-

fore a holy relic. There were relics beyond them in the fragrant astral darkness, incense made darkness astral, mosaic filled it full of
darting fish-gilt of gilt light. Mosaic glinted. They were safe under
water. They were in water, prenatal beings, un-born. The Kingdom
of Heaven is within you ... mind slit the thing to tatters. Pre-natal
come unto me all ye that are weary. They were weary, heavy laden
with intellectual burden. *Go preach the gospel* ... of beauty, mind
that slits dream from crass reality. "Dream is the reaching out feelers like a snail's horns. Reality is the shell or the thing of crystal
boxes. We must have the two together."

16

IF *go preach the gospel* was indicated so was *love one another.*
When Greek meets Greek in Saint Mark's Cathedral, Saint Mark's
Cathedral is another name for Delphi. *You have conquered O pale
Gallilean,* maybe, but there was another Gallilean waiting for them
in the moonlight. Moonlight made all of the Square a toy set there
by some ardent child, corridor and space before corridor and little
set of steps and columns set up carefully under arches. Saint Mark's
Cathedral was a child's pasteboard set of buildings, its toy village
done to this columned pattern, forgotten in a garden. It was true
that you could slit the thing to tatters, it had none of that quality Gareth liked ... reality. Standing in the outer doorway of Saint
Mark's Cathedral, Raymonde said to Daniel, "we must go back to
Gareth."

AFTERWORD:
H.D.'S RECITALS

ALTHOUGH H.D. is recognised primarily for the invention of Imagism and her contributions to the creation of modernist poetries, her serious readers have also long known her as a writer of prose. Like her contemporaries, James Joyce, Virginia Woolf, Gertrude Stein, Dorothy Richardson, Mary Butts, and Djuna Barnes, H.D. saw herself as working to break with the traditional forms of realism in the name of artistic freedom, to reshape fiction toward some active recognition of the terms of life as *she* encountered them. She published four novels and several novellas and short stories during her life. Several more novels including the three post-war novels she called her "Commedia" remained unpublished until recently because they were judged to be commercially unviable.

The stories in this volume were published during a period of intellectual ferment and introspection for H.D. "Narthex" came out in 1928, two years after her novel *Palimpsest,* written during the early years of her relationship with the film-maker, Kenneth McPherson. "Ear-ring" and "Pontikinisi (Mouse Island)" were published in 1932 and 1936, during the years of her analyses with Mary Chadwick, Hans Sachs, and Sigmund Freud. In the same period she published a number of other prose works including

The Usual Star, Nights, Mira-Mare and *Kora and Ka,* and *The Hedgehog,* a children's story written for her daughter. In her early 40s, she was revisiting and rethinking the events of the first half of her life, especially the three visionary experiences that occurred on her first trip to Greece[1], as well as the unfolding configurations of significant relations that followed on those extraordinary events.

H.D.'s prose has a very specific feel to it. It can be almost claustrophobic at times, especially during this period of her writing, locked into a mode that rarely concerns itself with descriptions of either a natural or social world. Like Virginia Woolf in *The Waves* and Gertrude Stein in *Three Lives,* H.D. was concerned to recreate an experience of mind at work in language. Like Woolf and Stein she approached mind in language through a kind of static dynamic (or dynamic stasis) and in forms of repetition which reinforce that, which is to say, nothing much seems to happen, though it happens with a great deal of energy. There is the unwinding sense of a slowly transforming sentence toward a revelation of deeper meaning, but little in the way of, say, "character development," a key element in the traditional realist novel. In so far as there are events, they are mental. But whereas both Woolf and Stein (and Joyce and Faulkner) located in their writing a social world not unfamiliar to the novel as literary form (even as they transform their vision of it), H.D. never quite did. With Woolf, you get glimpses of an English world full of the faded grandeur of disappearing Empire. With Stein you get glimpses of a young American black girl's physical and social location at the turn of the century. But rarely did H.D. give you even that much, partly because to do so would have been to enter the world of the novel.

The novel (and the short story as an offshoot of that) as a form is tied historically to a mode of perception or understanding that itself reflects a mode of being contracted or restricted within the thought of a singular material world. It has been a laboratory for theorizing the Lockean individual and its relation to Comptean "society" within the parameters of a world of matter in motion. Much of the 19th Century was spent grieving that as a terrific loss while revelling in the new forms of self, space, and time brought into play by it. By the 20th Century, the grief gave way to an exploration of the new freedom and an explosion of new forms. But Joyce, Stein, Woolf, and Faulkner, for all their radical deformations, never step out of that cosmology. In some ways, those writers' freedom with conventions signalled the end of (the authority of) those conventions, their imminent transformation into something completely different. In other ways, though, it endorsed the limits of those forms. *The Waves, Ulysses, Three Lives,* and *The Sound and the Fury* all push the idea of individuality into contortions of linguistic enactments of mind, but they never abandon the cosmology in which that individual is crucial to its order and the limit of its knowledge. Different senses of psychology, one of the central "human sciences" that theorizes the dynamics of the individual self, dominate the various attempts to present that self in language. And psyche's defining twin, its perpetual dancing partner, is always something called "society," which is understood as an existential limit determined by the various tyrannizing opinions and hierarchies of relation that make up a world of individuals.

H.D., even in her most "realist" prose, was never concerned to represent that dimension of experience. Instead she came back to certain events, certain moments, a certain array of selves that she circled around, or in on, as if with each pass she got closer to something that they embodied. These are not "social" lives, "social" selves, or "social" situations. These are powers, active images of nodes of meaning, unfolding constituents of a cosmos full of meaning, and the writing is a way of returning them to their original meaning where that "origin" is always here. In some sense, the writing takes place outside time, or rather, in terms of H.D.'s own experience, introduces the Image to time, while simultaneously introducing time to the Image. Moving away from the limiting identification of herself as "Imagiste,"[2] an identification that led to a measure of recognition but quickly became confining, she used prose to loosen the stasis of Image while maintaining the hierophantic intensity of Image to move the sense of time out of some relentless historical progression. This was the extent of her move "away" from Imagism. In the intensifications that arose out of this new arrangement, the world was (re)constituted as textual deferral in the continual reading and rereading of the events and persons that defined the parameters of her life. Events, in other words, were seen as a text with an esoteric, inner meaning that was accessible through exegesis. But reading was inextricably tied up with writing, and so the repeated recitations yearn after a closer and closer relation to the image extension of the moment – exegesis as a return to meaning.

She must say something. The only thing that vied, in clarity, with debit and credit, and the idea of numbers ruled on paper, was a flight of silver, that was yet a violin that, with all its exaggerated and emotionally timed rise and fall, swept over their heads, out to the bluer aether. With it, as she watched it, were those sharply defined impressions of columns, cut against blue, against violet, against deep violet, against purple, as the sun sank beyond Lycabettos. Lycabettos rose like a ship about to set sail, Hymettus rested like a ship in harbour. Only the Acropolis remained static, itself a harbour, an island above a city, a city set on a hill, an idea that, in all its eternal and remote dimension, still cut patterns in the race mind, the human consciousness, now murky with din and battle, as that violin's rhythm and sway, cut pattern across fumes of countless cigarettes, the dreary reiteration of a thousand diplomats. She must hold on a little longer.

In this moment from "Ear-ring," as the recital proceeds to intensify, Archie Rowe, for example, becomes far more than a mere boor, a bourgeois socialite. As the columns of debit and credit of his imagination are resolved into the columns of the Acropolis, he is revealed as voice of the social itself, the debit and credit dimension of the world that demands attention, "murky with din and battle," even as the music of the writer's song reaches after some other "columns" and the eternal patterns they cut in the mind. Madelon is equally more than an artist on a trip to Greece with her friend. She is the embodiment of an ancient desire for what lies beyond, just as the Russian woman is more than she seems:

> Madelon looked at the girl frankly, but now saw her as something, again, different. But what she saw her as she could not yet say. Was the Russian woman doomed, by some law deeper than the social law of gossips and of diplomats? Were rigorous laws functioning here, laws far older than the Norman Conqueror, the authentic county inheritance of the head of the British school, at work here? Was there some vein of mystery, some occult knowledge that they all shared? Was mid west right to ignore Salamis, except as a stepping-stone to oil wells, and was little Allie (upstairs sleeping) protected and forewarned, when some authorised academic snob purloined her pen knife from

her? Could they, even today, dig too deep? Was it wise to penetrate below a surface that the British school so carefully kept in its place, that an opera-bouffe royal family had the wit and courage to ignore, that Archie Rowe, with a mother from Achaea, went to Oxford expensively to forget?

Even the diamonds become more than diamonds as the recital reaches its "climax" and become a doorway into a new "layer," a new dimension:

> Don't look at the diamond. Eleanor is shuffling her feet and I'll have to wait till Rowe, tediously, takes leave before, upstairs, I can burst into this new layer, this new discovery, before I can tell Edd, or E.E., as I have learned to call her, how she can paint pictures like that. This is the new music. Everything seems unrelated yet diametrically related, as you slant one facet of a diamond into another set of values.

H.D.'s "fiction" is often referred to as *roman à clef,* "a novel that represents real people," *The Bedford Glossary of Critical and Literary Terms* says, "in the guise of novelistic characters bearing fictional names." You can read H.D.'s work in these terms. No doubt the characters that circulate through these stories began as "real people." She did return to the same persons in her writing, often under the same names, as well as to the same events. They have been identified many times: Gareth, Raymonde, Katherine, Daniel translate into Bryher, H.D. Gregg, McPherson, Pound, Gray, Aldington, McAlmon, and so on, the people who constituted the meaningful relations of her life. The stories included in this book involve the usual suspects and, in "Pontikinisi (Mouse Island)," a familiar event, sometimes referred to as "the stranger on the boat" story. But in another sense the definition of *roman à clef* begs the question since the terms it uses are all obscure or contested – "represent," "real," "fictional," and "character," far from having clear meanings, are the sites where high modernist fiction waged its struggle with realism, H.D. no less than Joyce or Woolf.

Beyond that, the idea of the *roman à clef* itself is usually connected to some sense of caricature or satire, some social commentary or critique that makes the "representation" of "real people" significant beyond mere gossip about who was sleeping with whom (although that is invariably of some interest) – Huxley's *Point Counter Point,* for example, or closer to (H.D.'s) home, John Cournos's *Miranda Masters,* in which H.D. was presented in a less than flattering light. But that is not what H.D. did in her fictions. There is no sense of caricature or satire in her writing. Nor is there the necessary fascination with what we call the "social" which is a prerequisite for that.

On the contrary, H.D. seems interested in undoing the ground of such a possibility by turning language toward an original intensity that is commensurate to her experience of a world bursting with sense, thriving with forms, beyond the social, with an inner truth that shines through the things of the world – the world as "Pear Tree,"[3] or, as in the story "Ear-Ring," diamond:

> ... she wanted something, unrelated to time, related to infinity, to communicate with something unrelated to time, related to infinity.... You related time-out-of-time, to time-in-time and you get snatches of each, in bits of jagged-off triangles.... It was the sharp edge of a cut-off triangle that must be the one facet of that diamond. That must be each facet of a diamond that was a new way of thinking.

This deep concern was what fuels her transformation of imagism into narrative. This turning of language was the defining element in H.D.'s perpetual, metamorphosing quest in both her poetry and "fiction" and had nothing to do with the impulse behind *roman-à-clef.*

This process was not unique to H.D. One of the closest descriptions of it is given by Henry Corbin in his discussion of the recitals of Avicenna and other Arabic visionaries. The process is called "ta'wil" and it operates within a very specific sense of the world:

> *Ta'wil* usually forms with *tanzil* a pair of terms and notions that are at once complementary and contrasting. *Tanzil* properly designates positive religion, the letter of the Revelation dictated to the Prophet by the Angel. It is to *cause the descent* of the Revelation from the higher world. *Ta'wil* is, etymologically and inversely, to *cause to return,* to lead back, to restore to one's origin and to the place where one comes home, consequently to return to the true and original meaning of a text.

The point here is the sense of a depth and dimensionality to the world that yields to exegesis. Call it *esoteric* compared to the world we live in during the rush and clamour of a day – the literal world that seems to end at a singular explanation, and yet contains within it access to further meanings waiting to be unlocked, unfolded. In such a world, each person who radiates in your life bears further meaning in the folds of their selves. In "Narthex," Raymonde, Daniel, and Gareth, all characters in other fictions, other recitations, are embodiments of powers struggling to become legible, a "hieroglyph language" she calls it. Recognizing they are part of that language, Raymonde comes to see them in a new light, so to speak, accomplished through the recitation a new state of being.

Growing up in Pennsylvania in the Moravian Church, H.D. early on had the example of Count Zinzendorf, the 18th century leader of the Church, to guide her sense of this "hieroglyph language." Zinzendorf, who took over leadership of the Unitas Fratrum (the original name of the Moravian Church) in 1723, initiated a cult of the Wound within the church, a radical feminizing and sexualizing of Christ's body that captivated H.D. Although the church later rejected Zinzendorf's vision, H.D saw in this moment an eruption of the knowledge of the perennial cult of love that reappeared in pagan Mystery religions, Dante's love cult, erotic troubadour mysticism, the Cathars, and the cult of the Madonna. The Moravian Love Feast, as their service was called, could be added to this list, in name if not in action.

Zinzendorf also developed the notion of "the church within the church," the formation of an inner circle of initiates and devotees who would maintain the original (esoteric) mission of Christianity in the face of its corruption by a profane world. In an essay on her own work, "H.D. by Delia Alton," H.D. specifically mentions Zinzendorf's plan and relates it to a further lost, or inner, history that her work engages:

Zinzendorf had re-established a branch of the dispersed or "lost" Church of Bohemia. This Church, to my mind, shows marked traces of the still earlier dis-established or "lost" Church of Provence, the Church of Love that we touch on, in *By Avon River*. The fascinating subject of the Hidden Church, the Church within the Church is touched on in "The Secret," the section of The Gift that reveals the child's affinity and actual connection with the old Jednota of Bohemia, or the Unitas Fratrum as re-established by Zinzendorf, across the frontier in Saxony.

This sense of an inner and outer reality to "life," an exoteric and esoteric dimension, was not concerned with the "social" other than as a text from which to initiate a movement beyond it.

A word, a foot-step or a sea-wind fluttered banner … waft of fresh scent, heliotrope in boxes, everything changed everything … wisteria pulled off a wall in passing, stuck in an under-mannered tourist's coat flap … the eyes of Miss Smithers from Newcastle-on-Tyne, Daniel who sat unmoved, yet fully sensed it. Raymonde had only to say "Veronese," "balcony" and she knew he saw what she saw. Hierograph … beating in the air, dot and tick and tick and dot of super-sensuous language … the flutter-ing of the streamers of the a-symmetrical symmetry of the lion banner, the tilt of a summer sun-shade, the fluttering of a pigeon … everything means something, a candle on a candlestick, a bird pecking at a brioche … heaven is getting things (thoughts, sensation) across in some subtle way, too subtle to grasp with intellectual comprehension … this hieroglyph language she and Daniel had between them.

In this writing where "heaven is getting things across," everything has meaning, meaning that unfolds in the "characters/real people" of the writing, whichever dimension you address them in, all ci-phers of something else, some further meaning that is explicated by being written and rewritten: "… the … *ta'wil* … is not an al-legorical exegesis," Corbin wrote in *Creative Imagination in the Work of I'bn Arabi,* "but a transfiguration of the literal texts, referring not to abstract truths, but to Persons." H.D. was never interested in the historical dimension of the novel nor its conventions the way Joyce or Woolf or Faulkner were, even though, like them, she went after the formal conventions as a way of freeing the energy of the (evolving) form toward her own ends. Her writing has nothing to do with the traditional concerns of the novel (or short story). These persons are not characters nor is this Newton's (or Einstein's) space or time. The space of this writing remains the soul and the time is the time of time itself. The social is a (largely opaque) abode within it.

These three stories are visionary recitals in that they *are* the passage of the soul from one level of experience to another, one level of reality to another, where a further sense of meaning reveals itself – where vision expands, grows into new astonishing spaces. They are full of that sense, but it is never completed, never contained, never finally deciphered. Beyond it, for those who are interested, are hints of even larger, more intricate spaces, which they adjoin. In a description of another collection of her stories, H.D. wrote: "…they are individually separate, dedicatory Chapels or Chapters…. They are Chapter-houses, adjoining some vast Cathedral." Her work opens into this Cathedral, an opening that remains unique to her writing among all her contemporaries.

Michael Boughn
Toronto, 2011

SOURCES:

1 After being abandoned by her lover and nearly dying in the flu epidemic of 1918, H.D. was rescued by Winnifred Ellerman (Bryher). After nursing

H.D. back to health, Bryher, the daughter of an English shipping magnate, took H.D. and her newborn daughter, Perdita, on a cruise to Greece and Egypt. During the course of the trip, H.D. had three visionary experiences which she wrote and rewrote in a number of different texts. On the way through the Greek Islands, she encountered a Guide in the form of a fellow passenger who showed her a vision of dolphins. This is referred to as the man on the boat story. Later, on the same trip while in Corfu, she saw a series of images on the hotel wall, and then witnessed a series of visionary dance scenes with Bryher.

2 H.D. first gained notoriety as a poet when at Ezra Pound's suggestion her early poems were published in 1913 in *Poetry* under the name, "H.D., Imagiste." She became identified with the movement called Imagism and her poetry was seen as quintessentially imagist.

3 "Pear Tree" was one of H.D.'s early Imagist poems in which she pushed language toward an intensity that bursts with a sense of the world's inner meaning.

COLOPHON

Manufactured in an edition of 500 copies in the fall of 2011.
Distributed in Canada by the Literary Press Group: www.lpg.ca.,
and in the USA by Small Press Distribution: www.spdbooks.org.
Shop online at www.bookthug.ca

BOOK
PRODUCTION
WAR ECONOMY
STANDARD